THE DEAR

His Lordship regarded Liz with an amused affection.

She was a tall, slender girl who appeared taller because she wore no crinoline. Her dress was black with a white collar and cuffs which gave her a quakerish appearance and her dark brown hair was dressed in a coronet of plaits, an unelaborate style which had the effect of emphasising the fine lines of her head and neck. Her eyes were a deep greyish-blue and set under rather heavy brows which gave her a serious air.

The Dear Colleague

Frances Murray

CORONET BOOKS
Hodder Paperbacks Ltd., London

Copyright © 1972 by Frances Murray
First published by
Hodder and Stoughton Ltd., 1972
Coronet edition 1974

Printed and bound in Great Britain for
Coronet Books, Hodder Paperbacks Ltd,
St. Paul's House, Warwick Lane,
London, EC4P 4AH
By C. Nicholls & Company Ltd,
The Philips Park Press, Manchester

I SBN 0 340 18293 8

1

From the small salon of Lacombe House there came the
sound of female voices joining in a lugubrious hymn.
Andrew the footman glanced across at Mr. Baker the
butler whose face was stony with disapproval. The hymn
trailed to an uncertain close and the voice of Mrs.
Frobisher boomed out through an inch and a half of solid
oak in the extempore prayer which had cost her two hours
at her escritoire that morning. The studied periods were
interrupted by a peremptory knock at the front door. The
two servants sprang to attention and Andrew opened the
door with a flourish. The owner of the house, Lord
Lacombe, strode in and immediately the echoing spaces of
the hall appeared to contract. He was a grizzled man in
his early sixties who gave the impression of an enormous
and barely curbed energy. He handed his grey Jolliffe
shallow to Baker while Andrew waited to take the old-
fashioned, caped driving-coat which was bedewed with
November drizzle.

"Wretched day," commented his Lordship.

The occupants of the small salon began another even
more lugubrious hymn and their unwitting host winced.
"Good God! What's that?"

"The Society of Ladies Devoted to the Provision of
Bibles to Native Persons, my Lord," replied Baker without

expression. "They generally open their meetings with a short service of prayer and praise."

"If that is praise," said his Lordship acidly, "I wouldn't want to hear them abuse anyone."

"No, my Lord."

"Where is Miss Liz?"

He made for the door of the library followed by Baker. The butler coughed and laid his hand on the doorhandle.

"Miss Elizabeth was not desirous of attending the meeting," he informed his Lordship.

"Small wonder."

"She requested me to inform Mrs. Frobisher, should enquiries be made for her, that she was not to be found."

"You mean she's gone out? In this mizzle? The girl must be about in her head."

"No, my Lord."

Baker opened the door.

"The arrangement was that I should not look for her. I apprehend the young lady is working here, my Lord. Perhaps if you were to look in the far window ..."

"Quite, quite. Thank you Baker."

His Lordship did not have far to look. The library was a large L-shaped apartment, warmed by a fire at either end. Here he found his ward, Elizabeth McLeod, perched on the library ladder and evidently engrossed in a Report of the Proceedings of the Committee set up to Enquire into the Provision of Railway Communication between the towns of Halifax and Hull.

"There you are, m'dear. I need a helpin' hand as usual. Can you spare a few minutes?"

She replaced the bundle of papers and stepped down from the ladder.

"Of course, sir. A pleasure."

His Lordship regarded her with an amused affection.

6

She was a tall, slender girl who appeared taller because she wore no crinoline. Her dress was black with a white collar and cuffs which gave her a quakerish appearance and her dark, brown hair was dressed in a coronet of plaits, an unelaborate style which had the effect of emphasising the fine lines of her head and neck. Her eyes were a deep greyish-blue and set under rather heavy brows which gave her a serious air.

"Got a speech tonight. Important. Johnnie Russell's gone to Windsor to see the Queen and taken Palmerston with him and the Tories have tabled a Question. Somethin' about the Turks. They've been cuttin' throats again ... or gettin' their own cut. Have to get at the rights of the matter. Pam tells me he sent some stuff round from the Office this morning."

Elizabeth frowned and looked along the line of boxes on a lower shelf.

"That'll be the Smyrna affair, I dare say. There are the Ambassador's Reports. The copies arrived from the Foreign Office this morning. And there were copies of some other letters from Athens. Pam's comments in the margin might be useful. I'll find them."

His Lordship cleared a space on the cluttered desk and took a sheet of paper from a drawer.

"I want to write to Hector. Must catch the post. I'll do it while you're rummagin'."

He unearthed a quill and began to cover the sheet with his bold handwriting. The point softened and dragged so he took out his pen-knife and began to mend it.

"Saw young Enderby's brother at the House this morning," he announced. "He says the boy's well on the mend and he'll be back with us in a day or so."

Elizabeth looked up from her search.

"I'm glad to hear he's better, very glad, but in a way I'll be sorry not to be able to help you any more."

"Nonsense," barked his Lordship, "No work for a girl, this. Ought to be out enjoyin' y'self, not stuffin' in here among the papers."

She bent her head over the file of letters.

"Oh, it's just that I shall miss having a rational occupation. I've enjoyed these last few weeks."

"Enjoyed havin' you, m'dear. Don't have to spell out things to you. You're blessed quick to take m'meaning always."

"You're very kind."

"No more than the truth, girl. And your gift o' tongues is amazin'. Fact is, I'd be obliged if you'd write me the occasional letter and so forth, even after Enderby's back. He can construe Homer like the ancient Greeks but his French is shockin'."

"It will be a pleasure, sir."

He peered at her.

"I believe you mean it, hey?"

"I do."

"Just the same ... you're a girl. Ought to be gaddin' about meetin' people. Findin' a husband, y'know. It's no use to you writin' letters for an old fogey an' all this prayer an' praise and the devout ladies and the parsons for tea."

He glowered at her.

"Couldn't stand it myself. Don't. Dine at m'club as often as not. You've got to stand the nonsense and look pleasant."

Elizabeth swallowed and nodded.

"I do miss having someone to talk to about normal things," she admitted, "I mean things which haven't any-

8

thing to do with the Church and the services and the sermon. And I miss having a proper task. I kept house for my father and I acted as his secretary, as I told you. Perhaps it's really that I miss him. We were so ... so friendly. That's a silly word for what we were really. After my mother died he took me with him everywhere. There was always so much to do and to see. I grew accustomed to being busy."

His Lordship cleared his throat.

"Well, that's understandable. And this I will say, he trained you well. I'll miss you when Enderby comes back. He's a nice lad but not overly well-endowed up here."

He tapped his forehead.

"But it wouldn't do, y'know, it wouldn't do. Not proper, y'know. Not in m'dotage yet."

"I know."

"Y'won't be in your blacks for much longer, hey?"

"No, sir."

"M'sister'll have to take you about a bit. I'll have a word with her."

He caught her looking at him with a raised eyebrow and an unmistakable twinkle in her eye. He laughed aloud.

"Take it you can't see Jane doin' the pretty, hey?"

"In a word, sir, no."

Lord Lacombe flung down the pen.

"You're right, of course. Dammit, girl, I'm at a stand. Y'father asked me to look to you. Gave m'word I would."

"But, sir, I'm sure he didn't mean—"

"I know what he meant, all right and tight. He meant me to see you respectably married and settled. You'll never meet a *parti* going to prayer meetin's and Exeter Hall and singin' hymns."

9

"I'm sure he never intended you to tease yourself like this. I've found the material you want I think."

"Good. Ah, good girl. Just what I need."

He skimmed rapidly through the papers for a few minutes underlining and making notes in the margin while Elizabeth thumbed through another file. Suddenly he flung down the quill again.

"And you're not all my worry, y'know. Here read this."

He took a letter out his pocket and handed to her.

"That boy of mine got himself in a mess. It's all over Paris that he's got himself mixed up with a married woman. She's run off from her husband. In Paris of all places. He'll find himself with two people and one breakfast behind the Tuileries one of these mornings. Shouldn't tell you, but wanted to tell someone."

He stripped the feather from his quill and watched her anxiously while she read the polite elliptic phrases of the Ambassador's letter. She looked up and smiled at him.

"The gist of this letter seems to be that he can't be spared at this stage of the negotiations or H.E. would send him packing. Also it would seem to be more of a rumour than a full-blown scandal."

His Lordship grunted.

"He's a good boy, Hector, knows his job and enjoys it."

He tapped the letter in front of him.

"I've sent for him to give him an earwiggin', though Lord knows what good that will do. He's a man of thirty now, not a school boy. If he takes some nonsensical notion into his head talkin'll pay no toll."

"I'm sure he must listen to you, sir."

"Oh, he'll listen. He'll let me talk m'self to a stand and then go his own way in the end of all. Silly young clunch."

He heaved a sigh which rattled the papers on the desk and then addressed himself again to the material she had found. They worked on after that with Elizabeth in her neat, clear hand pinning down the telegraphic phrases which he jerked out at her.

In the servants' hall Baker and Mrs. Morpeth the house-keeper, who was in legal fact an angular spinster, were refreshing themselves with strong tea and buttered muffins in a corner secluded from the rest of the servants.

"The mistress is fit to be tied," announced Mrs. Morpeth, not without satisfaction.

Baker looked at her over his tea-cup and decided that she had a particularly juicy morsel to impart.

"And what has come up her back this time?" he enquired.

"His Lordship and Miss Elizabeth," she said portentously. "She thinks that Miss Elizabeth is setting her cap at his Lordship and wants to turn the Mistress out of doors."

Baker stared. Mrs. Morpeth nodded.

"Allardyce said she was muttering away about designing hussies and being turned out in her old age to starve."

"I wish I might see the day," said Baker with feeling. "Pudding-faced old ..."

"Mister Baker, please; remember yourself."

He gave her a calculating glance.

"The mistress may be his Lordship's sister," he pronounced, "but she is a fool ... and no lady if she thinks that."

Mrs. Morpeth sniffed in agreement.

"As if his Lordship would," she commented, "a girl like that. Her relations are cottagers on some Scotch island at the back of beyond. They don't even speak the Queen's English."

11

"They say," she went on, "that her father was a trooper in his Lordship's regiment."

"'They' are right for once," said Baker, "Sergeant McLeod he was, and they spent the war saving one another's lives, by all accounts. McLeod nursed the Master through dysentery on board ship coming from the Americas."

"That's as may be," said Mrs. Morpeth.

"Mr. McLeod was a great man," Baker reproved her, "and he was a gentleman, a real gentleman."

"A common engineer," she sneered, "and a railway engineer at that. Dirty, smoky, smelly things."

"*But* profitable." Baker reminded her, "Miss Elizabeth will have one hundred thousand pounds of her own."

"A tidy sum," admitted the housekeeper and coughed.

"It's six months since Miss Elizabeth's father died," she remarked, "She'll be going into half-mourning. In fact ..."

She raised her eyebrows meaningly.

"... the 'person' who waits on her ..."

"Catriona," interpolated Baker with a smile.

"Outlandish name. She told Allardyce that the dresses came home from Pugh's this morning. White and lilac, she said, with black ribbons."

"Very proper," approved the butler and sipped his tea.

"Mrs. Frobisher," said the housekeeper thoughtfully, "is not one to let the grass grow under her feet, as you might say."

Baker wiped butter from his upper lip.

"We will have a guest for dinner tomorrow night," he said. "Andrew was sent to Mr. James' lodgings with a note this afternoon."

"Ah," breathed Mrs. Morpeth.

Baker put his cup down with a clank in the saucer.

"And when his Lordship hears about it," he added, "there'll be two people fit to be tied."

In this he was quite right. Next day when Lord Lacombe was informed that his nephew was to grace the dinner table that night he muttered something unprintable under his breath and sent Andrew scurrying for his hat.

"I'll dine at m'club m'dear," he said to Elizabeth who was replacing the litter of books and papers on the library desk, "Can't bear that whinnying ninny. Puppy!"

On which rather confused note he departed. Elizabeth was soon able to commend the accuracy of this description. James Frobisher was an undistinguished young man. He suffered from a lack of height combined with a tendency to put on weight. In an attempt to make his mark among his contemporaries he had adopted all the fashionable eccentricities. His neckcloths assumed amazing dimensions, his whiskers were combed and pomaded into the forefront of fashion and he made great play with a monocle of plain glass which he screwed in and out of his eye socket with monotonous and irritating frequency. But all this was nothing to his speech which was liberally strewn with the modish catchphrases and in which he contorted his vowel sounds out of all recognition. A's were flattened out of existence, u's became a's, and he had by constant practice acquired the fashionable lisp.

Elizabeth entered Mrs. Frobisher's sitting-room where the family usually gathered before dinner expecting a chilly reception for she knew herself unforgiven for not attending the meeting of the previous day. Instead, her hostess put aside her embroidery and hastened to make herself agreeable.

"You can have no notion, James, what pleasure it has given me to have this dear girl in the house. It has made me young again, I declare it has."

Elizabeth managed to conceal her surprise at such a

13

speech. From her own observation this pleasure had been well-hidden by an all too apparent irritation. Her hostess and she agreed lamentably seldom on what constituted appropriate occupation for a girl of nineteen. Elizabeth regarded the covering of altar-cloths and cushions and bell-pulls with elaborate embroidery in virulent colours without enthusiasm and preferred to read avidly in the excellent library, extending an education which Mrs. Frobisher considered already unbecomingly extensive. Nor could she display any of the demonstrative piety required by her hostess whose devotion to the Anglican Church was marred only by the regularity with which she quarrelled with the vicars in the many churches round about.

In view of this it was understandable that Elizabeth was unable to make any coherent reply to this declaration.

"That inconsiderate brother of mine," continued Mrs. Frobisher with a terrifying playfulness, "has been keeping poor Elizabeth a positive prisoner in the book-room, James."

"A scandal, 'pon m'soul, a cwying scandal!" exclaimed her son, "A pwetty pwincess in dithtwess, what?"

"She has been so occupied with my brother's letters and speeches this past few weeks since young Enderby suffered his accident that I've hardly seen her. I've been quite neglected, haven't I, you naughty girl."

She shook a playful finger at Elizabeth who was still too stunned at this mode of address to reply.

"'Pon m' soul ... letters and speeches. How vewy tedious, Miss Elizabeth. You mutht have found them quite intolewable."

"On the contrary, Mr. Frobisher. I was grateful for the chance to make myself useful."

"Surely you have not been denied opportunities of making yourself useful since you came?"

14

A touch of acid broke through the sugar in Mrs. Frobisher's voice and James hurried gallantly into the breach.

"'Pon m'soul, it's hardly work for a gel ... I mean to say, dreary politics, what? Ethpethially a pwetty gel."

"While you are in Town, James, I hope you will find yourself able to take the child out of herself a little."

"A pleathure, Mama, a twue pleathure."

Mrs. Frobisher turned toward Elizabeth.

"Of course balls and evening parties are not eligible just at present until you have put off your black ribbons, but I have arranged ..."

She paused and heaved a deep sigh.

"... I have arranged for my dear friend, Miss Leadbitter, to chaperone you. If only my health would permit me to have this pleasure myself."

Mrs. Frobisher devoted what time she could spare (and it was much) to her health. Healthy as an east wind she had persuaded herself that the indigestion which resulted from a combination of overeating, tight-lacing and no exercise was the symptom of a weak heart. She patted her black satin bosom and continued, "There is a private concert of sacred music at Mr. Messiter's house and Mrs. Lamond is giving a literary soirée ..."

Elizabeth stole a glance at James' face and bit her lip at his horrified expression.

"... both of these would be perfectly eligible. Then my good friend Mrs. Gorsuch has promised to send cards for her private musical evening. Her nephew has been studying music in Germany and is to be giving a pianoforte recital."

James swallowed hard and broke in on this catalogue.

"Er, Mama, would it not be ... could Miss Elizabeth not go to the play perhaps?"

His mother considered this revolutionary proposal in

majestic silence for a moment while Elizabeth smothered a regrettable temptation to giggle.

"In no circumstances may she attend a comic performance. Shakespeare's tragedies, perhaps would be permissible, or some other elevating and moral piece ..."

Luckily for Elizabeth's composure this dismal list of festivities was interrupted by Baker's announcing dinner. It was however, only a temporary respite. Though Mrs. Frobisher's plans for her entertainment were extended over the soup by a lecture on the Antiquities of Egypt, a public reading by a wellknown author of his Essay on the Economy of Nations and an exhibition of paintings of religious subjects the conversation was soon dominated by her son who regaled them with interminable accounts of the witticisms with which he had favoured his friends and how they had received them with tears of mirth, a circumstance which gave Elizabeth a very fair notion of his friends.

Once again, she was rescued by an interruption. Lord Lacombe stumped unceremoniously into the drawing-room, glared with unconcealed distaste at his nephew and was thanked, nervously, for his hospitality.

"Pleasure, m'boy, pleasure," he barked impatiently and untruthfully. "Evenin', Jane. Glad to find you still below stairs, Liz, m'dear, I need a hand. D'ye mind?"

She rose with relief and turned to her hostess whose face had become an alarming plum-colour.

"Of course, sir. If you will excuse me, Ma'am?"

Mrs. Frobisher's answer was, perhaps luckily, drowned in her son's protests.

" 'Pon m'soul, Uncle, the poor gel ... t'ithn't the act of a gentleman I do declare ..."

His uncle took no notice but held the door for Elizabeth. Following her out he shut it with what might have been termed a slam. Once in the library he grinned at her conspiratorially and pointed to a tray by the fire.

"Madeira," he announced. "Wouldn't hurt a kitten. Care to join me?"

She accepted a glass.

"What is it you would like me to do?" she enquired. "I collect you have just come from the House. Did they slap down a supplementary?"

He laughed at her and waved his hand at the chair on the other side of the fire.

"Nothing of the kind. Thought you might be in need of respite, y'know. Perseus to Andromeda, if m'memory serves me."

"It's a comic monster. More a Caliban," she remarked.

"He's harmless enough," said James' uncle and his tone condemned that young man utterly, "but one evening of his company can drive me near an apoplexy."

"I was in some difficulty," she admitted, "I was trying not to laugh."

She rehearsed the dismal course of dissipation outlined for her by his Lordship's sister and described James' reactions to it until her listener wiped his eyes and begged her to stop before he was carried off.

2

It became evident that Mrs. Frobisher had decided that the neatest and most economical way of ridding herself of the threat to her position as chatelaine of Lacombe House was to marry Elizabeth and her hundred thousand pounds to her son. Miss Leadbitter, a thin and fluttery female, whose lifework had been the care of a demanding parson father, placed an unexpectedly liberal interpretation on her duties as chaperone. Elizabeth found herself, all too often, thrown into the almost undiluted company of James. He enlivened the exhibition of pictures of religious subjects with an interminable monologue concerning the glories of his Hampshire estate. At the literary soirée he vidently considered the readings of verse and prose to be very poor entertainment for he provided a *sotto voce continuo* of stories about his misfortunes at the race course until he fell asleep during an essay on the significance of the now defunct Chartist Movement, read by an earnest young Scot. For a time this came as a relief until he began to snore in the most embarrassing fashion. Elizabeth, not without a certain satisfaction kicked him viciously upon the ankle. At this he plunged awake with an oath which made their neighbours stare in virtuous indignation.

Warned by this experience, Elizabeth forebore to waken her escort during their visit to the play and she heard Macready play Macbeth through a duet of snores from

18

Miss Leadbitter on one side and James on the other which somewhat diminished her interest in the performance. She described this circumstance to Lord Lacombe who spluttered briefly with laughter and then enquired whether there was any post as he had not as yet had any answer from his son.

One afternoon, a week after young Enderby had returned to his secretarial duties, Allardyce, the plump and harassed elderly maid who attended Mrs. Frobisher was sent to Elizabeth's room with a note. In a flowing hand Mrs. Frobisher informed Elizabeth that dear James had asked his mother's permission to take Elizabeth to view the pictures at the Royal Academy. Miss Leadbitter was awaiting her in the small saloon and James would call for them both at two o'clock.

Elizabeth had an uncomfortable sensation that the visit to the Academy might well provide a setting for the dénoument which she had seen approaching for some days. For a craven moment she wondered whether she might plead a headache but soon concluded that this would only postpone the difficulty.

They had not been in the Gallery for long before Miss Leadbitter declared that her feet would carry her no further and that she would rest for a space on the seat before the picture of the dear little Princesses. However, this was not to prevent dear Miss McLeod from enjoying this interesting exhibition to the full. James who was unexpectedly well-acquainted with the rooms lost no time in leading her into a small side-room which was graced by a series of very ugly female portraits. It was a room which was, and seemed likely to remain, deserted.

"I thay, perwaps you'd care to thit down, Miss Liz,"

suggested her escort, "Doocid hard on the trotters, art, eh, what?"

He handed her to a wooden bench from which the ugly women could be viewed in appropriate discomfort. Elizabeth resigned herself to the inevitable. James, somewhat disconcerted by her uncompromising silence seemed to be having some difficulty in broaching his subject.

"I thay, you do look weally handthome in that lilac wobe," he began at last.

"You are very kind," said Elizabeth with chilly formality.

"Oh, not at all, my fwiends thay I have vewy good tathte," he observed. "I alwayth thay I thimply could not abide to mawwy a dowdy female."

Elizabeth smoothed out the creases in her gown.

"Let us trust that you find someone who lives up to your exacting standards, Mr. Frobisher," she said sweetly.

This was a mistake because irony was lost on him.

"Well ... I hope ... that is ... you know you have the motht exthellent tathte, Miss Liz, quite unextheptional, plain y'know, but everything elegant. Y'have thtyle, Miss Liz and I alwayth thay it ith thtyle that countth."

"Indeed."

Silence fell between them. James coughed and then breathed so deeply that Elizabeth could hear the creaking of his stays.

"Er, Miss Liz?"

"Yes?"

He stared into his hat as if he had a copy there of what he was about to say to her, and it was apparent from the first sentence that his speech had in truth been conned beforehand.

"I fully wealithe that it ith not long thinthe your thad loth," he rattled out, "and I mutht make the thtrength of my feelingth my excuthe for appwoaching you tho thoon. I can only hope that my adwetheth at thuch a time may not be unwelcome."

At this point he stuck fast and stared hard with bulging eyes at the ugliest of the females in front of them as if he hoped for inspiration there. Elizabeth looked down her nose and concentrated on restraining the mixture of irritation and amusement which rose in her. James swallowed hard and noisily as if screwing himself to the uttermost.

"I er ... I er, er," he stammered and then struck his stride again. "During the patht weekth I have come to admire you motht thintherely and I cannot let another day path without telling you of the emotionth you have routhed in my breatht. I have spoken to my mother and athked her permithion to pay my addresses to you and she was pleased to give me permission."

Elizabeth, struggling with her laughter noted that the lisp was beginning to lose the battle.

"You might have done better to ask your uncle," she suggested, "he is, after all, my guardian, not your mother."

This seemed to put him out a trifle.

"My uncle?" he said, "but surely if my mother approves he can have no objection to the scheme?"

"You may be right," said Elizabeth with a manifest lack of conviction.

"Well, anyway," he continued conscious that his peroration had been somewhat marred, "I would be most honoured if you would consent to become my wife."

"Really, Mr. Frobisher, you take me rather by surprise," she replied conventionally if a trifle untruthfully.

"I realithe that there has not been much time for you to become accuthtomed to the idea, and I do not preth for an immediate reply," he continued (and it was clear that he had managed to return to his script) "I fully understand you might not in the thircumstances find yourself able to return the regard which I have for you. However, I hope I have your permission to ask my uncle to pay my addresses to you."

It was Elizabeth's turn to draw a deep breath.

"I think it would save us both a great deal of embarrassment if you did not," she said firmly.

He stared at her open-mouthed.

"I do not think we would suit, Mr. Frobisher, and I doubt if I would ever find myself able to return the regard you profess to have for me."

She rose and shook out her lilac skirts in the hope of ending the interview as quickly as she could.

"Our tastes are not the same and I feel we have too little in common," she added.

"But, Miss Liz...."

"And my name," she reminded him with emphasis, "is Elizabeth, Elizabeth McLeod."

He stood up reluctantly for her height gave her a certain advantage over him.

"Miss Elizabeth, please, don't go ... you cannot have considered fully ... our acquaintanceship is so recent ..." he persisted, "Perhaps if I were to wait, perhaps a few months might see a change in your feelings ... your recent bereavement ..."

"I don't think that my sentiments are liable to alter, Mr. Frobisher. And now I must return to Miss Leadbitter, she will be wondering what has become of us."

The chaperone was watching for their return with a sentimental smile upon her face from which Elizabeth deduced correctly that she knew very well what had become of them. The smile faded and the words of congratulation which were hovering on her lips died when she saw

Elizabeth stalking down the gallery while Frobisher trotted behind her like a scolded pup.

It soon became apparent at dinner that James, in telling his mother of the episode, had suppressed certain important facts. Mrs. Frobisher, in oppressively good humour, made arch references to a future which implied that Elizabeth was to be one of the family, but which were too oblique for Elizabeth to disillusion her without being blunter than would have been polite. His Lordship, dining at home for once, was preoccupied by his son's failure to reply to his letters and heard perhaps one word in ten spoken by his sister, thus missing the implications completely. Towards the end of the meal Mrs. Frobisher was forced to come out into the open.

"And what do you think of such a happy connection, brother?" she enquired with an unction which set Elizabeth's teeth on edge.

James went scarlet and gobbled something unintelligible. Elizabeth did not know whether to laugh or to lose her temper once and for all. His Lordship was quite patently at sea.

"Connection! What connection?" he barked.

Mrs. Frobisher's lips thinned.

"You must have remarked the growing understanding between Elizabeth and dear James," she asserted acidly.

"What? Stuff and nonsense. She wouldn't have him," returned his Lordship brutally and departed leaving a distinct atmosphere behind him.

James, encouraged by his mother, persuaded himself that Elizabeth had rejected his suit in a momentary access of maidenly modesty from which she was bound to make a recovery. He wrote a laboured poem to her blue eyes, set to an Irish tune, which he sang to her with a languishing emphasis which at any other time she would have found hilariously funny. As it was she indicated primly that her eyes were actually grey and it would be better if he dedicated his poem to his mother whose eyes were, in fact, a pale and irascible china-blue. This suggestion was welcomed as a daughterly attention by Mrs. Frobisher who presided over these rites with an overwhelming benevolence.

Lord Lacombe on encountering his nephew, as it seemed to him, in every room in the house, became more short-tempered than ever. He dined, predictably, at his club and signified his disapproval of James with a choleric and unnerving stare whenever he encountered him.

It was thus something of a surprise when one evening he appeared in the small drawing-room after dinner. He discovered James reading from a volume of Byron's poems while his mother embroidered an altar-cloth and Elizabeth presided over the tea-tray wishing fervently that the conventions permitted the use of arsenic as a solution to social dilemmas. His Lordship interrupted a Byronic flight unmercifully.

"Ah, Jane, glad to find you still up. I want you to dine some people," he rapped out. "This Thursday."

"But, Lacombe, you must know that I never hold dinner-parties," she said, on a rising note of indignation. "My health does not permit it."

"I know, I know ... don't mind as a rule ... like m'dinner in peace and quiet."

He cast a meaning look at James who was endeavouring to whisper in Elizabeth's ear, an exercise which, as her ear was at least six inches above his own, involved him in some ludicrous exertions.

"I'll give Elizabeth, here, the names and she can write the invitations for you," he announced.

"But I repeat, Lacombe, it is out of the question."

Mrs. Frobisher's voice was a trifle shriller than usual but her brother took no notice.

"The food'll need a bit of thought, m'dear. Two of them are Indians of a kind and of course they'll not eat beef. The others are Turks and they won't eat pork. Religious scruples, y'know."

Mrs. Frobisher rose to her feet, her bosom heaving with a mixture of emotions.

"Religious scruples! Do you mean to tell me that you wish me to invite heathens to my table?"

The vibrato in her voice at the word "heathens" was impressive but her brother was impervious.

"Why not, m'dear? 'I was a stranger and ye took me in', eh? Thing is, m'dear, we want to turn them up sweet ... shan't trouble you with the reasons but the order's out. Every consideration and hospitality *ad lib*."

"I will not permit it. I have a positive aversion to such people."

"Then you must overcome it, m'dear. Shouldn't be too difficult. They have overcome their aversion to you."

Mrs. Frobisher's face became purple and her brother hastened to explain.

"Not their custom to dine at the same table with females. Dislike it. Customs vary, y'know. So the least you can do is preside."

"I categorically refuse. It is too much."

His Lordship took a sip of his tea.

"Delicious, m'dear," he complimented Elizabeth. "As to that, Jane, you must please yourself. Elizabeth can preside for me if you choose to sulk."

There was a thunderous silence.

"Oh, and bye the bye, no wine. More religious scruples. And I expect they'll like their coffee sweetened to a syrup in the Turkish style. Elizabeth can show Guiseppe how to do the trick. They are all great nobs in their own country so we've got to butter them well."

James had got to his feet some moments earlier and had been gobbling feebly like a kettle on the boil.

"Sir, you are too high-handed, 'pon m'soul. I'll not have my mother tweated in this thtyle."

His Lordship rose and replaced his cup on the tray.

"Boy!" he thundered, "as long as your mother lives in my house at my expense she must endure my whims ... just as I endure her relations. Goodnight to you."

When Andrew returned from delivering the invitations the humbler members of the staff crowded round him to discover what he had learned of their exotic visitors. This was little enough but it was sufficient to throw them into a flutter. The Indians he informed them in bloodcurdling accents would be accompanied by armed retainers who would stand on guard outside the house while their masters dined within.

"Great big fellers wiv cloffs on their 'eads," said Andrew, "an' swords that long, ready ter slice bits off yer."

The effect of this was all he could have wished and Mrs. Morpeth was forced to restore order.

Mrs. Frobisher appeared in the large saloon to receive her guests dressed in purple satin with a ruby and diamond cross disposed ostentatiously upon her bosom. In her hand, to counter the arguments of the Infidel, she carried a vellum-covered Testament. Thus, armed at all points and supported by her son, she awaited the arrival of the strangers with all the enthusiasm of Mary Stuart awaiting execution.

It was not a successful evening. James' sole contribution was a powerful *sotto voce* observation called forth by the discovery that the ruby liquid in his glass was raspberry vinegar. His Lordship on making a similar discovery made a similar comment.

"Good God, Baker! What is this unspeakable ullage?"

Baker who had served it with a stony face and a bosom heaving with apprehension came to the head of the table.

"Mrs. Morpeth suggested . . ." he said basely.

"Take the damn stuff away and . . ."

His Lordship swallowed the end of the sentence with an effort.

"I feel," he said with marked restraint, "that water will be more acceptable to most of us."

In this he was right, except in the case of the Persian interpreter who drew a look of incredulous horror from his host when he asked for more and drank it as accompaniment to a ragout of lamb.

At Mrs. Frobisher's end of the table conversation languished. Few dinner-table trivialities can survive translation into two languages. Moreover, matters were further complicated by the interpreter's apparently not having eaten for a week, so that such commonplaces were percolated indistinctly through a wide selection of the entrées. Mrs. Frobisher made a few majestic observations concerning the weather and listened to the Urdu and Turkish renderings with an expression of outraged incredulity as if she were certain that the Persian was causing her to utter blasphemies. Sentences addressed to herself concerning the weather and the great city of London she examined as if they were strange and possibly dangerous insects before baring her porcelain teeth in daunting acknowledgement at the original speaker. It was unfortunate that owing to her inability to distinguish between her be-turbaned and be-bearded guests, and the slowness with which the process of translation proceeded she usually honoured the wrong speaker. The recipients of such marks of attention choked, gulped and fell silent, afraid that in some way they had trespassed.

After the second course had been removed with an excellent galantine the company by mutual (if unvoiced) consent gave up all attempt at communication and addressed themselves exclusively to the food in the hope of hastening the end of the ordeal. In this they were frustrated by the Persian who, deprived of employment, seemed ready to indulge indefinitely an inordinately sweet tooth. He looked up from a third portion of a caramel cream which he had found especially delectable to meet a glare of concentrated hostility from his employers. He then broke into a light sweat and finished his plateful with a speed which ended in an attack of hiccoughs. Mrs. Frobisher then looked majestically at Elizabeth and rose.

"We will retire, Lacombe, and leave you to your wine," she said conventionally and somewhat tactlessly.

As she followed in Mrs. Frobisher's wake Elizabeth thought she detected a perceptible lightening in the expressions of her neighbour and the two Indians. This was not lost upon his Lordship who raised a quizzical eyebrow upon his guests and beckoned to Baker.

In the drawing-room she went at once to the pianoforte and began to play the popular Irish melodies which were to Mrs. Frobisher's taste. This served the double purpose of preventing conversation and soothing the savage breast in the accepted way. By the time the door opened to admit James, his mother had so far relaxed as to beat time inaccurately upon the arm of the sofa.

It was immediately clear that James was in none too happy a frame of mind. His plump face was pink and his rather loose mouth clamped into an expression of mulish bad temper. He interrupted Elizabeth's playing without ceremony.

"Thwown out! I declare, turned out like a schoolboy! 'Pon m'soul it'th too much, too much!"

His mother made sympathetic noises and Elizabeth plied him with coffee.

"They started jabberin' ath thoon ath you left, doin' the polite, y'know, and then Baker brought in the decanterth ... all wubbish about not touchin' wine ... 'pon m'soul it ith. Lappin' it up, thtill are, confound 'em!"

He swallowed a scalding mouthful of coffee and choked on a mixture of coffee and spleen.

"An' then m'uncle thaid ... I'd jutht filled m'glass ... 'put that down, boy, and run along and join the ladies.' Ath if I wath about theven! I thaid thomething, at a loth, y'know, in front of thothe damn nativeth, and then he thaid ..."

His voice rose.

"He thaid, 'Dammit boy, ye came to thupport yer mother, go an' thupport her!'"

His expression of outrage was so ludicrous that Elizabeth was forced to turn hastily away and return to the instrument on which she began to play again while Mrs. Frobisher joined with him in abuse of Lord Lacombe.

After a while it became apparent that the subject of their conversation had changed. Elizabeth noted that their voices had dropped so that she could not hear what was being said and that there were occasional glances in her direction. Mrs. Frobisher began to gather together her fan and her Testament and rose to her feet. The expression on James' face was that of a swimmer preparing to break the ice on a lake. Elizabeth decided to move quickly.

She rose and closed the instrument.

"If you would both excuse me," she said, "I would like to find a book before I retire to my room. I wish you both a very goodnight."

Before either James or his mother could protest she was out of the door and pattering down the marble staircase. From the dining saloon came the sound of voices in an animated chorus. Wine, forbidden or not, had evidently loosed tongues. Lord Lacombe's laugh boomed out. Elizabeth heard the door of the drawing-room open.

"Nonsense!" said James' mother, evidently capping a reluctant hound to a scent, "No time like the present. No doubt you will find her in the library."

Elizabeth considered her line of retreat. The library was obviously out of the question and the morning-room with its door to the passage at the back of the house lay across the exposed and echoing spaces of the hall. Just at hand the door of the small saloon lay slightly ajar and from the glow within it was plain that a fire had been lit there.

She slipped inside but she had hesitated a second too long and James treading gloomily down the stairs had seen the whisk of her white skirts as she vanished. Inexorably he marched into the small saloon and found Elizabeth facing him apprehensively.

The small saloon was almost in darkness. There was a lamp turned very low on a small table beside the fire and the flicker of the firelight itself.

"Ah, Miss Elizabeth, I was hoping for a word with you." he greeted her and closed the door firmly behind him.

"I was just about to go upstairs," she protested, "surely the morning would be more suitable ..."

"Not more than an inthtant, I athure you," he insisted. "All I want is a few momenth."

"Just as you please."

She clasped her hands in front of her and reflected that

there was little point in postponing what promised to be an uncomfortable scene at any time. Having thus gained her attention her suitor seemed somewhat uncertain how he should continue.

"Er, will you not be theated?" he suggested and indicated one of the two armchairs which flanked the fireplace.

"If you are not to be long, I would prefer to stand."

Elizabeth knew how much he disliked the fact that she was taller.

"Er," he said, "er, you may wemember ... we had a conversation at the Academy ..."

"I remember," replied Elizabeth crisply.

"I wath wondering, er, whether, er ..."

"Yes?"

"Whether, now you have had a week or two, whether you ... have thought any more ..."

"Thought about what?"

He swallowed hard.

"About the, er, pwopothition I made to you."

"You have been at some pains to keep it before me."

"Perhapth, you have reconthidered your anthwer," he suggested. "We thought if you were to have a little time ..."

"If I were to consider it for a year my answer would be the same," she told him firmly. "No."

"You would have an ethtablishment of your own," he pointed out, "country ethtate, all that kind of thing. Houthe in Town. Another thing," he continued, apparently deaf, "that houthe of mine, going to wack and wuin, I pwomithe you, needth a good mithtweth. You could furbish it up, new furniture and furbelowth, plenty to do down there."

"I suggest you employ a competent housekeeper."

"Oh, come, Miss Liz ... vewy fond of you, give you

m'word. Never offered for anyone in m'life. Athure you of that. Would make me the happietht of men ..."

"In that case I am sorry to have to disappoint you," she said briskly, "but I still do not wish to marry you and would be obliged if you would not tease me on the subject. And now may I go upstairs?"

Frobisher did not move.

"But why?" he insisted. "It would pleathe everybody. M'mother would be in tranthportth. My uncle would have you off hith handth and you would be comfortably thettled. What have you got againtht the thceme?"

Elizabeth took a firm hold on her temper.

"Please believe me, James, we would not suit."

"Why not?" he demanded petulantly.

"Because we have virtually nothing in common," said Elizabeth bluntly. "My upbringing and background are quite different to that of the females with whom you are acquainted."

"But Good Heaventh, Miss Liz, I don't wegard your, er lack of, er, birth. I mean one would never wealize that you ... that is ... In any cathe no word of weproach about your welations would ever path my lipth. After all they are not on the doorthtep prethithely, are they? I mean, don't have to athk them to dine, what?"

"That," said Elizabeth repressively, "was not exactly what I meant."

"Wath it not? Oh, well, jutht the thame," he went on, "it'th thomething you might wememper."

"Oh, I will," she said. "You may depend on that."

She moved towards the door.

"Now don't wun away," he protested. "It'th a perfectly eligible match. You mutht give me a pwoper weason for thwowing me over."

"Please let me pass," she asked.

"No, I thay, dammit," he said with a sort of feeble irritation, "we can't jutht leave it at that."

His eyes narrowed and he looked malicious.

"I thuppothe you think you can wait for a better offer?" Elizabeth lost her temper.

"You want reasons, you shall have them," she said icily. "Let me tell you I would not willingly spend an hour in your company, let alone a lifetime. Your conversation is vapid, you have not two ideas in your head to rub together. You are all but illiterate and proud of the fact. You have never done a day's work in your life and you seem to think this is a proof of your gentility."

"Well, weally ..." he spluttered in the face of this comprehensive attack. Appropriately enough, a coal had blazed up in the fire during this outburst and there was light enough for her to see the expressions on James' face. Outrage and astonishment gave place to spiteful fury.

"Illbwed little cat!" he flung at her, "How dare you! If you think you'll get a better offer than mine, you're wrong. Not many people would want to marry a low spitfire. Let me tell you even all your money won't make people of family swallow a mob of peasants calling cousins with them!"

"Not unless they happen to be as deep in debt as you are!" she retorted contemptuously.

He went purple in the face.

"I see that my mother was right," he said petulantly. "You are determined to marry my uncle."

She stared at him speechless, as if he had struck her a blow in the solar plexus.

"Well," he continued, "I'll tell you to your head, he'll not do it. You'll not wheedle marriage out of him for all your bookishness and your letter-writing and your foreign tongues. Oh, he might have made you his mistress ...

33

you're not the first since my aunt died, not by a long chalk . . . but he won't marry you. Oh, no!"

Elizabeth slapped his face as hard as she could and James staggered back from her holding his cheek.

"You bitch!" he gibbered at her. "Just you wait till my mother hears of this!"

Into Elizabeth's mind there flashed a picture of a small boy running for comfort to his mother's lap. She laughed aloud. This was the last straw. James turned at the door and fired a parting shot.

"My mother thinks you're his mistress, you know! And I believe her."

The door slammed and Elizabeth turned away burying her face in her hands.

"O Dhia," she lamented aloud, "my wretched temper. Oh, what a thing to happen."

From behind her she heard a movement and a slight cough. She whirled about and found a tall figure standing in front of the fire. He turned up the lamp and regarded her with a mixture of amusement and embarrassment.

"Well, you certainly gave him pepper, didn't you?" he remarked and held out his hand, "I'm Hector Lacombe, very much at your service."

3

Elizabeth, speechless with shock, put out her hand automatically.

"I am profoundly sorry," the newcomer said, "but there was really no help for it."

Elizabeth turned her back, unable to look at him.

"You see I arrived while you were dining," he explained, "I didn't want to interrupt, so I had Baker bring me something to eat in here. When I had finished I fell asleep. I have been on the road for thirty-six hours."

He put his hand on her arm and tried to make her face him.

"I am truly sorry," he apologised, "but you must see I could hardly break into such a scene once it had well begun. I woke *in medias res,* so to speak. I was just going to get up when, er, the ... the tone of the exchange, er, altered, and I thought it could only make matters worse if I emerged from my ambush at that point."

Elizabeth laughed rather harshly.

"It's hard to see how matters could be worse," she said. "My father always said I would fly into a rage once too often ... and he was right."

"You had sore provocation," he suggested. "I was surprised you remained civil as long as you did."

"It's no excuse," she said, more to herself than to him, "because he ... because I ..."

There was a gleam of amusement in Lacombe's eye.

"It was a mismatch in more senses than one," he put in. "Dear Cousin Froggie was a trifle outweighted, I feel."

"How ungentlemanly of you!" she returned. "But how shrewd. I feel as if I had beaten a baby."

She gave a shaky laugh and pulled herself together. Hector took her gently over to the fire.

"You know, you should sit down," he told her, "it was an ugly, little episode and you look to me a trifle shaken by it."

He put her gently into the chair which he had vacated and poured her a glass of wine from the decanter on the tray. She sipped it, still in silence. He sat down on the chair opposite and watched the colour come slowly back into her face. Elizabeth's thoughts were still confused but afterwards she remembered thinking that he must have taken after his mother, for, apart from his height and build there was little of his father about him, unless it was a certain decisiveness. His eyes were a clear hazel and his colouring dark, unlike the blue-eyed Saxon fairness of his Lordship and his sister.

"Feel more the thing?" he enquired after a minute or so. Elizabeth nodded.

"Good. I suppose you must be my father's godchild. He wrote to me that your father ... that you had come to stay here."

Elizabeth's hands clasped together round the glass.

"I have proved myself rather a difficult charge," she remarked drily.

He laughed.

"My father did not appear to think so. He called you a 'good little soul and no trouble to anyone'. I had pictured you with your hair down your back, working at your needlework."

"And now you find an abandoned woman with designs upon your father," she said, "it must come as a decided shock."

"Stuff!" he protested, "Don't forget I have known cousin Froggie for more than twenty years and am aware of the value of his opinions. And I know my father too well to believe anything so fantastic of him."

He glanced at her as she sat stiffly in the chair.

"Besides," he added, "even in this short time I think I have your own measure."

"You are very good," she muttered.

He realised that she was not far from tears.

"I was more sorry than I can say to hear your father was dead," he said. "You know he was my godfather?"

"Oh, yes," she said, "you were named for him after all."

"Of course. I wonder are we related in some abstruse style? Does one have god-brothers and sisters?"

"I don't know," she said and smiled at him. "It would be pleasant to think so. I always wanted a brother."

"You know," said Hector, thoughtfully, "I always wished I could have known your father better. I remembered the last time we met . . ."

"That was in Rome, wasn't it?" she interrupted eagerly, "We were there for the Mastroanni contract. He told me how you introduced him to the Count who had the quarry he wanted for the stone revetment, and how you smoothed the old man down and persuaded him to talk business even though he was the son of forty generations of counts."

He laughed suddenly. "The descendant of forty counts needed the money very much," he told her, "and he knew I knew it."

"Just the same, he was very pleased. He said you would have a remarkable career."

"That same career is somewhat in the balance," he admitted, "that's why I'm here."

"I know."

"You know?"

He sounded stiffly indignant.

"Your father told me."

"Did he, by Jove! Did he tell you why?"

"Yes."

He got to his feet and stood staring down at her.

"It would seem that my eavesdropping tonight was a kind of poetic justice," he said coldly. "I take it, you learned this while you were . . . how did my dear cousin put it . . . 'wheedling' my father . . ."

Elizabeth said nothing but rose and faced him, her face white and set. He made a gesture with the hand nearest her.

"I am sorry," he said with sincerity, "that was unforgivable of me."

"It's of no consequence," said Elizabeth stiffly. "It was natural you should think . . ."

"Nothing of the kind," he said. "It was unkind and unmannerly. I should have known better. My father's no fool. He knows whom he can trust. It's just that . . . it's a devilish situation. A tender place you might say." His mouth twisted sardonically. "I hope you will forgive me."

"There is nothing to forgive," said Elizabeth.

"Forget I ever said it," he begged, "for I assure you I never believed it."

"I have no experience of brothers," said Elizabeth, "but my limited knowledge of them leads me to understand that they may say what they please to sisters."

She smiled at him and held out her hand.

"Good girl," he said and grasped it firmly, "You know, our acquaintanceship progresses with remarkable speed. Within a few minutes we have come to know one another's most intimate concerns and now we have had our first dispute. It is disconcerting to consider where we may have arrived by tomorrow."

"Alarming indeed," she acknowledged. "And now I think I must go to my room. It has been a somewhat difficult evening."

"I cannot doubt it."

His eyes were alight with amusement.

"I am only sorry to have added to the difficulties ..." he began.

The voice of Mrs. Frobisher interrupted them. It was apparent that she was descending the staircase.

"She is in the small saloon, you say. Very well, I will speak with her myself, and tonight. Such conduct cannot be allowed to pass. It is beyond all things. Good night, James."

Hector seized Elizabeth by the arm and looked around the overcrowded little room.

"It seems that the difficulties are not yet over. You are being tried high, tonight. Quickly, get behind those curtains! Be careful not to let your dress be seen. Thank heaven you are not a slave to the crinoline. There! Now, don't move whatever she may say. I'll lie like ... like a diplomat, I promise you."

She found herself thrust behind the heavy maroon velvet and heard the whisper of wood on carpet as he dragged a chair across to hide her feet. The curtain billowed alarmingly as the door opened and then Mrs. Frobisher's voice boomed out only a few feet away.

"Miss McLeod! I insist upon a word with you! I must demand an explanation of your indecorous and ungrateful behav ... Hector! What is this? When did you arrive?"

39

"A short while since, Aunt. Baker told me you had guests so he gave me a tray in here."

"You could have given us warning of your arrival. I am very much put out by this kind of hole-and-corner conduct. You have no consideration at all. Just like your father!"

"I am sorry, Aunt . . . but it was uncertain whether I could leave until the very last moment."

"Fiddlesticks, the sheerest affectation. How should you be so occupied?"

"As you say, Aunt," agreed Hector drily.

"But I was informed . . . my son told me . . . where, may I ask is Miss McLeod?"

"Miss McLeod?"

"Is she not here? I wanted a word with her. Most particularly I wanted a word with her. Has she gone to her room?"

"I really could not say."

"But I was told she was in this room. My son said . . . how long have you been here?"

"A matter of an hour or so I suppose."

"And you haven't seen my son, or this woman?"

"I think I may say I have not yet seen James."

"It is all very puzzling. I am sure I was not mistaken."

"No doubt, Aunt."

There was a slight pause.

"Have you heard of your father's latest whim?"

"I have not yet had any speech with my father. He is engaged with his guests."

"Guests!"

There was a wealth of meaning in that syllable.

"Did he not write and tell you he had undertaken the guardianship of Sir Hector McLeod's daughter? You must remember him: the railway builder. A Scotchman. Such an unsuitable friendship for a man in your father's position I always thought."

"He was my godfather," Hector reminded her, "and a most remarkable man."

"He was once most uncivil to me. And why he should inflict his daughter as a charge upon me and my poor brother, I cannot comprehend. She would have been far better among her relatives in Scotland."

"Surely her father was the best judge of that."

"Oh, he wanted her to marry above her ... *and* she is doing her best to oblige him. Oh, yes, I make no doubt he would be proud of her."

"You are cryptic, Aunt."

"I tell you, she is a sly, pert, underhand, scheming creature. A forward, underbred hussy. I have borne more than enough at her hands and so I intend to tell her. Where is she?"

"She does not appear to be here."

Elizabeth, stiff with rage and embarrassment, could not help smiling at such a masterly prevarication.

"She abuses the hospitality of this house in a way I hesitate to describe."

"I feel sure you will overcome your hesitation, however."

The note of amusement was lost on neither of his listeners.

"So you find this entertaining, do you?" asked his aunt in a thrilling contralto. "Let me tell you, this abandoned creature has actually been setting her cap at your father. He means to turn me out and install this ... hussy in my place."

"You must be mistaken, Aunt."

"After I have done my best to become a second mother to her. To guide her and help her overcome the disadvantages of her breeding. She has spent most of her life

41

abroad without the benefit of genteel society. She is most farouche."

"Indeed," remarked Hector.

"And as if that were not enough my poor James must develop a *tendre* for her. Imagine my feelings!"

"I find it hard to imagine James in the grip of the tender passion, I admit," said Hector.

"Despite my feelings as a mother I put no obstacle in his way. The circumstances being what they were I thought it best ..."

"Her portion must be considerable."

"This," said Mrs. Frobisher indignantly, "is too much. You'll remember what I have said when you see a girl young enough to be your daughter, become your step-mother."

"I must have been a precocious twelve-year-old."

"That is a most indelicate remark!"

"And yours is a most indelicate suspicion," he returned, "or it would be if it weren't utterly ludicrous."

A third voice was added to the exchange.

"Hector m'boy! Baker said you was come. At last! Welcome home, welcome home! And what is so ludicrous, eh?"

"My aunt has a notion that you are going to marry Miss McLeod."

"Marry Liz! Jane, you're about in yer head!"

"I am not alone in holding this belief. The whole house-hold must think so by this time."

"Well, they're all a lot of ninnies and you are the worst of 'em. Go to bed, Jane, and try to see reason. I want a word with this boy of mine."

"I have long since ceased to expect either civility or consideration from you, brother, but ..."

42

"Good thing," said his Lordship. "Not my line of country, doin' the pretty. Not one of yer parsons."

"... but I refuse to endure gross incivility from your son. And you will send that McLeod creature from this house. If you do not, I will leave it myself and take pains to see that the world knows why I have done so."

"Do you mean you want me to send Liz away?"

"I do."

"Are ye serious?"

"I am."

"Why? The girl's done you no harm."

"Because her behaviour has been such that no respectable female could countenance."

"What?" exploded his Lordship. "What the Devil do you mean by that?"

There was a pause and then Hector spoke very quietly.

"I hesitate to tell you, but it would appear that my aunt believes you have made your ward into your mistress."

"Good God!" said his father, sharply. "Jane, you're not serious?"

"You have one day to make your choice," announced his sister portentously. "Either that creature leaves this house, or I do."

"Oh, go to bed, woman, and stop boomin' all over the house. I'll tell you what's to be done in the morning."

"Do you mean to tell *me* . . ."

Mrs. Frobisher's voice was appreciably shriller.

"I mean to tell you nothing till the morning. Go to bed. Goodnight."

There was a short and sulphurous pause and then the door slammed. Lord Lacombe let out his breath.

"Dreadful woman, m'sister, dreadful. An affliction. Now

m'boy we must talk. I asked Baker to bring us some brandy."

"But, sir, your guests?"

"Oh, they've gone. Settled the business in an hour. Decent fellow Selim. Speaks English very well after a few glasses of port."

"Father ... I ... Miss McLeod ..."

"Ah, yes, Liz. Pity she's got across Jane, but it was bound to happen. Chalk and cheese, chalk and cheese. Ah, the brandy, thank you Baker."

The butler who had been standing there long enough to prevent Elizabeth's emergence from her hiding-place, put the tray on the table and gathered up the dishes.

"I understand Mr. Hector has had one sleepless night already, m'Lord," he observed.

"Don't cluck, man. What d'ye think ye are? A wet-nurse? I won't keep him out of his bed very long."

As Baker closed the door softly behind him Elizabeth emerged from her hiding-place, feeling miserably foolish. His Lordship stared for a moment and then took her by the arm and brought her to the fire.

"Liz, m'dear. Where did you spring from?"

"I thought that Miss McLeod ..." began Hector.

"Her name's Liz," interrupted his father, "Elizabeth if you want. Fact is it's really something Gaelic which sounds like Yallersay but old McLeod assured me that it was Elizabeth in English. You'll be seein' a good deal of one another, brother and sister in a way, now, eh? Might as well use names and not peel eggs."

"Elizabeth, if I may ..."

Hector looked enquiringly at her and she nodded.

"Elizabeth ... er vanquished Cousin Froggie in here a little while ago. I heard some of the battle and it was a masterpiece. But James went straight to my aunt who came down breathing fire and brimstone and as Elizabeth did not feel up to an encounter ..."

Lord Lacombe grinned impishly and his eye went to the curtains.

"So you played hide and go seek, eh? Good as a play, b'jove," he commented. "I'll lay listeners heard no good of themselves, eh?"

"No sir," she admitted stiffly.

"Never mind, never mind. Damnably silly woman, m'sister, drum-headed. Just like my father. He could empty the House like a leaky bucket once he began speakin'. Had a bee in his head about the Catholics all wantin' to murder us in our beds, y'know."

His hearers found themselves unable to comment on this revealing anecdote.

"C'mon, girl, sit down. Glad to find you still below-stairs. May's well settle this matter tonight."

"Father! It's after midnight!" protested his son. "Surely the morning will be soon enough. Elizabeth must be tired."

"Stuff. Strong as a horse, aren't you, girl? No die-away nonsense about her," said his Lordship approvingly. "She'll sleep the better for knowing what's what."

He settled her in a chair and sat down himself, nursing his brandyglass. Hector remained standing, one arm on the chimney-piece and frowning down at the toe of his shoe.

"Yes, she's a damnably foolish creature, m'sister," reflected his Lordship, "and she's a schemer too in a stupid way. But, she is my sister."

He paused and looked keenly at Elizabeth.

"D'ye see, girl? If she leaves my house, and she meant what she said, make no mistake, it's bound to cause talk and it'll be unpleasant talk, and it'll reflect on you. Can't expect a silly creature like that to hold her tongue, and

45

she won't. 'Sides, you couldn't really stay on in this house when she wasn't here. Not with the kind o' tales she'll be spreadin'. See?"

"Very plainly, sir," said Elizabeth.

"Can't have that kind of talk," he continued, "promised yer father I'd have a care to you. Puts me in the devil of a fix."

"I see. I am very sorry."

Elizabeth's head was bent and her hands clenched in her lap.

"It's hardly her fault, father," Hector intervened suddenly, "All this to-do is because she won't marry Cousin Frog and you'd hardly expect her to marry my cousin merely to get you out of a fix."

"Not apportionin' blame, m'boy."

His father glanced sardonically at him.

"I was just gettin' at the bones of the matter. Wouldn't expect any girl to marry young Frobisher unless she was at her last prayers."

Elizabeth raised her head.

"Of course I must go, my Lord. I'll find some respectable woman to bear me company and set up my own establishment. I could find a small house in the suburbs, perhaps."

"No," said his Lordship.

"But how else can I . . ."

"At nineteen, you're too young by far to set up on your own. Yer father would turn in his grave."

"Then I will go to my people in Skye," she said quietly, "I am sure they will welcome me."

"I am sure they will," said his Lordship. "But you know very well that yer father didn't want that. He escaped it. He didn't want you to go back to it. He said so."

"But I wouldn't have to endure the poverty he knew. I wouldn't have to carry water and hoe potatoes and starve through the winter on meal and herring, as he did," objected Elizabeth. "I have enough to live very comfortably there."

"And just how would you live?" he challenged her. "Alone?"

She looked him full in the face for a second and then her eyes dropped.

"Precisely, you see what would happen as clearly as he did. You would be welcome for a week and suspect for a lifetime, and, I expect, milked for your money. You would fret yourself into an early grave for loneliness. They're good people, your relatives, but you would be out of place among them now, and what is more you know it."

There was a short silence, broken by Hector.

"Well, now you have her cornered, what do you propose?"

His voice was unexpectedly acid. Lord Lacombe raised his eyebrows at him for a second.

"No need to be so partisan, m'boy. I feel her situation as much as you seem to do."

Elizabeth stood up.

"As the situation is of my making," she said decisively, "the solution should be mine as well. Your responsibility for me was never more than an informal arrangement, my Lord, and you have discharged it beyond the call of friendship. I will never be able to tell you how grateful I am for all your kindness, and your care. I will travel north in the morning."

Much to the surprise of both Hector and Elizabeth his Lordship greeted this speech with a chuckle.

"Heavens, girl, but you are like yer father. His very tone and expression."

"I fail to see what that has to do with it," said Elizabeth stiffly. "I promised to come here because it was my father's wish and because I knew it would make his mind easy when he was ... while he was dying."

The last words were harshly spoken and her hands closed on the folds of her skirt as she recalled the scene; then she turned and faced him.

"But, my Lord, I am in legal fact my own mistress and I have no wish to remain when my presence has become a problem as well as a burden."

Once more his Lordship disconcerted them both with a chuckle.

"Come down from your high horse, girl, before you fall off. Your father knew you very well, better than you realized. He foresaw something like this, wily old fox."

Elizabeth stared at him.

"He said ... remember you went to fetch the sawbones when you had made your promise? ... he said then, that you could be hot at hand and thrust a packet of papers at me, all ready for my signature. Not because he didn't trust me, he said, but to give me a stick to beat you if you needed it. You know how he could be, dry as a desert. You're my legal ward, m'girl, till you're thirty or you marry a man of whom I approve. Show you the papers if you want."

This bombshell had all the effect he could have wished. Elizabeth sank back into her chair and put her hands over her face. Hector stiffened and put his glass down with a sharp click. His father glanced up and checked the angry comment on his son's lips with a frown and a gesture.

"Now, don't upset yourself, girl," said his Lordship comfortably, "there's more than one way out of this maze as you'll see, and you won't have to marry either James or myself. Not that I'd object, you understand, but it would cause a deal of talk. Do you mind if I smoke? Like a cigar, this time o' the night."

Elizabeth shook her head and his Lordship lit a fat cigar.

"Now, m'boy, your turn. Let's have a round tale from you."

Hector turned round indignantly.

"Father, you go too far."

Elizabeth rose quickly.

"I hope you will excuse me."

"No, m'dear. Won't keep you long, but we may need your help."

She stared.

"Mine? But how could I possibly ..."

He blew out a cloud of smoke.

"You'll see soon enough."

"Father, I must protest. Why should Elizabeth be loaded down with my problems? She has enough of her own."

"You know hers," said his father. "Only tit for tat."

"But ..."

"All in good time, boy. Go on, and don't miss anything out."

Hector shrugged and began, hesitantly at first. It was a straightforward story. He had met Eloise de Mavanne during his first year in Paris because her husband was a Government official and they encountered one another at various official receptions: but the acquaintance had been distant and formal. Four months ago he had heard in the normal course of gossip that she had run away from her husband and his only reaction was to wonder with whom she had gone and why she had not done so sooner. Like most of his acquaintance he cordially disliked de Mavanne. He had forgotten the affair until one spring day when he had met her in a very unsalubrious Quartier, trying to sell a ring.

D

"May one ask what *you* were doin' there?" asked his father.

"I have a very wide acquaintance in Paris," said Hector, "I find it ... informative."

"No doubt, m'boy, no doubt. Go on."

"The rogue of a jeweller swore it was stolen, refused to buy and said he would go to the police. He just wanted to beat down the price but she believed him, ran from the shop and cannoned into me because she was crying. She was hungry. I gave her a meal at a café and slipped some money into her bag."

Hector frowned into the fire.

"I was surprised when I found she was alone and without money, I admit, but that was all ... then."

"What made you seek her out again?"

"It seemed a good idea to keep an eye on her."

He glanced at his father.

"I'd become ... interested ... in her husband's activities. I thought she might be able to tell me something about them. What people had come to the house while she was there, that kind of thing."

"And could she?"

"Not at once. When I managed to track her down again, she was ill. She couldn't work. She'd been in a workshop making cheap dresses. She had no money left at all and she was going to be put out of her room. I think my arrival seemed a bit like the *deus ex machina*."

"So you paid her rent. I suppose we can deduce the rest for ourselves."

"No," said Hector. "It wasn't as simple as that. She was ill in September again and it was unbearably hot in that attic room of hers. I didn't go very often, just once in a while for a few minutes to see whether she was all right and to have a talk. I'd asked some ... friends ... to keep an eye on her, but dammit, father, she was lonely."

"Of course. Go on."

"I found her a room in a little inn outside Paris for a month or so. I had to get her out of the town. And I went out to see her there. She was so much better and it was pleasant in the country."

"And you were seen?"

Hector nodded.

"Luckily, it was someone who knew me but not her. She was terrified and insisted on hiding herself in Paris again. I didn't stop her because I'd been finding out a thing or two about de Mavanne. Do you remember that Deputy Charles Gascoigne who was found with his head beaten in?"

Lord Lacombe looked up quickly.

"You mean de Mavanne was responsible?"

"I wouldn't go so far as to say that. But Gascoigne had been investigating his department, and he had hinted at certain irregularities."

"Did Madame, what's her name ... Eloise ... couldn't she throw any light on this?"

"I hardly liked to ask her. But I had other sources of information. The trouble was they weren't very discreet, de Mavanne realised that I was coming rather too close for comfort."

"What I don't understand is why you wanted to come so close, as you put it. What business was it of yours?"

"What interested me was his connection with a certain section of the Orleanist party."

"Ah!" said his father.

"Ah, is all very well," said Elizabeth, "but I would like to know why this is so important."

"Because our respected Ambassador to France has a

certain understanding with the Orleanists. If they are making use of a man like de Mavanne H.M. Government could find themselves in a very nasty situation. If there was an attempted *coup d'état* for example," explained Lord Lacombe.

"I see," said Elizabeth. "Relations could be strained."

"Especially if it wasn't successful," returned Hector.

"Well, what about this de Mavanne, m'boy?"

"I think he wanted to start a scandal which would force Lord Normanby to be rid of me before I could find out any more. He accosted me in public, at a reception. He accused me of . . . well, you can imagine. He demanded to know where his wife was and generally created an unpleasant scene. But he wasn't sure enough of his ground to force a duel on me, especially in public. I'd say it was an inspired guess based on a description of the woman my friend had seen with me at the inn. Eloise is, well, striking in appearance."

"What did you say?"

"I lied as hard as I could," Hector flung at him. "I knew by then why she had left him and I wasn't going to risk his finding her again."

"Violent to her?"

Hector nodded.

"H.E. would be put about."

"He was. If I hadn't been necessary to the Turkish negotiations I think I'd have been sent packing. Just what de Mavanne would have liked."

"What's de Mavanne's attitude now?"

"Oh, he's made a form of apology. But I wouldn't trust him," said Hector. "And his accusations were based on a real suspicion, and he's still suspicious."

His Lordship grunted. Hector turned his back on the room and stared into the fire.

"Seems to me that there's nothing in this that can't be mended with a bit of discretion," said his father.

"You've not heard the whole," said Hector flatly.

Lord Lacombe frowned at the broad back.

"Go on."

"She's to have my child."

Silence fell, and then his Lordship sighed gustily.

"She told me just as I was going to leave for London," Hector explained. "She was ... unwell ... and the doctor told her ..."

"Here's a pretty kettle of fish. Boy, you are a fool. It's an idyll, I suppose."

"You might call it that."

His voice was totally without expression.

"And what do you think of all this, Liz?" demanded his Lordship suddenly.

"I?" she stammered, "Why ... I hardly ... it's none ..."

"Don't beat about the bush, girl."

Elizabeth drew a deep breath.

"I think ... I think he showed consideration and compassion," she said firmly. "It would have been easy enough to pass by on the other side, or salve his conscience with a bundle of banknotes and make her feel like a beggar."

"Consideration, hey?" interrupted Lord Lacombe leaning forward in his chair. "You call it consideration to take advantage of a woman in her position, to seduce her?"

"Don't talk fustian," she said angrily, and Hector turned around at the note in her voice. "There are times when it is kinder to take rather than to give. And what else had she to give?"

There was a startled silence. Hector looked at her as if for the first time and his Lordship considered her through narrowed eyes.

"It's an unexpected viewpoint to have from a gently nurtured female," he commented drily.

Elizabeth's mouth twisted as if she had tasted something acrid.

"That is a nauseous phrase," she said.

Both men laughed and she blushed.

"You asked me not to beat about the bush," she reminded them.

"I did not expect you to cut it down altogether," said Lord Lacombe and flung his cigar into the fire. "But you have cleared the ground, certainly. Now, m'boy, I take it that you can't marry the girl?"

"No," said Hector. "Out of the question. Even if he ... she is ... devout."

"Has she any family?"

"They disowned her. She ran to them first of all and then ran off again when they were going to send her back to him."

"And she obviously cannot go back now."

"It would kill her."

Hector's voice was calm but it was plain that he meant what he said.

"I don't suppose her present situation is known?"

"No."

"And it seems to me that your connection with her is more rumoured than proved. Is this correct?"

"As far as I can tell."

"Good. We can proceed on that basis. What are you going to do?"

Hector turned back to look into the fire.

"I would have thought it was obvious."

"Alas, yes. Just the same ... Liz, what would you do in such a case?"

Hector turned about sharply.

"I will tell you what I intend to do. I am going to resign my appointment and bring her back to England. We will live retired. I am here only to make the arrangements." .

"No," said Elizabeth emphatically.

They both stared at her.

"That may be the honourable answer to this problem," she went on, "but it is about the worst thing you could do. You will fret yourself to a shadow for lack of occupation and you will come to hate her because she was the cause of your leaving the Service. She will be miserably unhappy and the good Lord alone knows what will be the end of it all."

There was a charged silence and then his Lordship thumped the arm of his chair with a clenched fist.

"She is right, b'God, and you know it, Hector."

Hector flushed angrily.

"What if she is? I can't in honour do anything else."

Elizabeth stood up.

"I am peasant-born," she said, "and it seems to me that I cannot understand you people even if I have lived among you all my life. To commit a folly like that in the sacred name of honour when it will poison the life of four people at least. What is this 'honour'? A Moloch?"

"Four people?"

Hector looked bewildered. Elizabeth turned on him.

"Yes, four. Your own, hers, the child's, poor little creature, and your father's. Have you no notion of his pride in you, his hopes for you?"

"Do you think I haven't thought of all this?" he asked her, his voice tight and angry. "I tell you there is no other way ... none."

"And I tell you that you are too hidebound in your

55

wretched 'honour' to think clearly. There *must* be a better solution!"

Lord Lacombe broke in from his armchair. He was looking at them with some amusement.

"Now, now, the pair of you, squarin' up like a couple o' prizefighters. Sit down, Liz, and cool off. Hector, have some brandy and for Heaven's sake stop lowerin' over me like a thundercloud."

Rather sheepishly they both sat down and looked at him.

"Now," he said, "let us think about things and just to please you, Liz, we'll throw 'honour' into the discard."

He made a gesture with his hand.

"Right. One thing we must know."

He looked a trifle embarrassed.

"I am not in m'dotage yet, and Liz has made her views as clear as you could wish. How d'ye feel about this Eloise, boy?"

Hector did not answer at once. When he did it was without looking at either of them.

"I must see that she is ... well, safe and comfortable. I am responsible. The child is mine."

"Fair enough," said his father. "And how does she feel about you?"

"I told you, she is devout. The situation is ... difficult for her. She is in a state of sin."

Again Hector took a moment to think.

His father raised his eyebrows.

"She feels guilty?"

"She has not said so," said Hector, "but I have come to know her well."

"She would not go into a greensickness if you, er, ended the connection, then?"

"How can I 'end the connection' as you put it?" asked Hector indignantly.

"Dammit boy, you can look after the woman without makin' her your mistress, that's what I meant, savin' your presence, Liz."

Hector looked at his father frowning.

"I believe it might even be a relief to her," he said, "but, she is alone, she looked forward to my visits, even when, even if ..."

"Of course she did," Elizabeth put in forcibly, "in her place it would be kindness I would value, not ..."

She stopped hastily and went scarlet. His Lordship raised a quizzical eyebrow at her and chuckled.

"I hope I am too much of a gentleman to ask you to finish that sentence," he remarked.

"I hope so too," said Hector, smiling, "but Elizabeth has put her finger on the keynote of this ... this connection."

"As you say, m'boy."

He looked at them both.

"Well, we have the situation well defined now, no unspoken reservations, no prevarications. Surely we can find some happy solution? Come now, Liz, never known you at a loss yet."

4

Next morning Mrs. Frobisher received her brother in her boudoir. She had fortified herself by reading, not without relish, the ninth chapter of second Kings. Lacombe was unimpressed by the barricade of tracts and religious works which lay on the table before her. Characteristically he broached his matter without preamble.

"Well, Jane, we're to have a wedding next Monday," he announced, a piece of information which silenced his sister effectively. "I've set young Enderby to obtain the licence and so forth, and your man ... whatsisname ... Carruthers will perform the ceremony. Saw him an hour since. Nothing too elaborate of course with the girl's father not dead a year, but there'll be a few friends. Enderby'll be groomsman and Liz says she wants no attendants. Sensible girl that."

He laid a list on the table.

"I've scribbled a few names, add anyone you care to. Enderby'll attend to the invitations. No call for much in the frippery line. She'll get all that in Paris."

Mrs Frobisher's bosom swelled and she swept the list off her desk as if it were a dangerous insect.

"Brother! Have you taken leave of your senses? A girl young enough to be your grand-daughter, the daughter of a ... a ... a low ..."

She spluttered with fury.

"McLeod was one of the best men I ever knew," said her

brother. "His girl's good enough to marry anyone, or so you appeared to think yesterday."

She drew breath.

"Brother, if these are your plans I will take the train to Chalkston today. I won't stay another hour under this roof. I have borne much but this is too indecorous to countenance. You will in any case no longer require my presence after Monday. A few days unchaperoned will be neither here nor there in such a scandal as this match will make."

Lord Lacombe raised his eyebrows.

"Didn't require yer presence at any time," he observed bluntly. "It was you, Jane, who decided to come here after Mary died. Ye're free to go any time y'please. I'll direct Baker to order the carriage for you. Enderby can look out your train."

He sat unmoved through the tirade which followed this unfeeling speech and succeeded in stemming it by lighting a cigar which drove her, coughing ostentatiously, from the room. He then grinned wickedly and made his way to the bookroom. From the upper floor came confused sounds, feet scampering to and fro, doors slamming and over all the hubbub his sister's voice, volleying orders. Two footmen emerged from the basement carrying a dome-topped trunk between them and laboured up the staircase only to be halted by a scandalised Baker who indicated that they should use the back-stairs. The footmen vanished through the baize door at the end of the hall with the air of men who can barely restrain their feelings. Baker acknowledged his master's presence with a bow.

"I understand that Madam is leaving us," he remarked.

"Yes, Baker," said Lacombe cheerfully, "we will become a bachelor establishment."

A flicker of interest crossed the butler's face.

"Indeed, sir. Mrs. Frobisher would appear to be under a misapprehension."

"Well, well!" said his Lordship opening his eyes very widely. He vanished into the bookroom.

Hector was standing in his usual attitude one arm on the chimney-piece, staring into the fire.

"Mornin' m'boy. Slept well, I hope?"

Hector turned round.

"We can't do this," he said. "It's wrong."

"Thought you'd get cold feet, m'boy," said Lacombe, easily, "but you've overslept, y'know. There a notice gone to the *Mornin' Post* and another to *The Times*. They'll appear tomorrow. Enderby's off to get the special licence. I've seen the parson. It's all in train. I tell you we've been workin' this morning."

"I still say we can't do this to her."

"She agreed last night."

"I know," said Hector, "but she was worn to a thread what with Cousin Froggie, and then you went over her like a cavalry charge."

"If you think that, you don't know Liz."

"That's exactly what I mean," interrupted Hector, "I don't know her, and she doesn't know me."

His father ignored this.

"I hauled her off the train to Scotland at eight o'clock this morning. I heard her come down, heard the cab. Expectin' something of the kind so I followed her. Had the Katerin with her."

"There you are. It's obvious she doesn't like the idea. You can't just push on like this."

"We'll see."

His Lordship rang the bell and looked with distaste at the garish wool-embroidery on the bell-pull.

"Once yer aunt's gone I'll get rid of these devilish things," he remarked.

"Aunt's going?"

"Didn't you hear all the to-do? She's packin'. Doesn't approve of a weddin' in the family."

Before Hector could comment on this Baker came in.

"My compliments to Miss Liz, Baker, and ask her if she would step in here for a few moments."

When the door was shut he gave Hector a rueful glare.

"I never did want yer aunt here. We never could agree. Thing was, I couldn't be rid of her. Kept on prating about blood bein' thicker than water. Frobisher left little but debts . . ."

"But I don't understand," said Hector, "she's got a comfortable home with you here. Why should she leave you just because Liz is getting married?"

Lacombe looked faintly sheepish.

"Thing is, m'boy, I didn't explain that she was gettin' married to *you*. Yer aunt's got a bee in her head about Liz and me any way. I just let it buzz."

"But if she goes, Liz can't . . . she must . . ."

"Just so, m'boy, just so."

There was a charged silence.

"It may be unfilial in me to say so," observed Hector quietly, "but you are a barefaced, unscrupulous, scheming blackguard."

Lacombe responded to this reading of his character with a blast of laughter.

"Wouldn't be in the F.O. if I wasn't, boy."

Elizabeth arrived in time to hear part of this exchange. She was pale and looked underslept. Hector placed a chair for her and she sat down without looking at him.

"Ah, Liz, m'dear. Had some breakfast?"

She nodded.

61

"Good. Nothing like breakfast to make the world seem a better place. Now let's get this sorted out. Why the cold feet, eh?"

Elizabeth glanced swiftly at Hector, found he was looking at her and bent her head.

"For my part," said Hector, "I think it unfair to marry Elizabeth off to a man she has met once, simply because her presence in your house has become a problem."

"Not her presence that's the problem. It's yer aunt's absence."

Hector shifted his shoulders impatiently.

"You know perfectly well what I mean."

Lord Lacombe looked across at Elizabeth.

"What are your views, girl?"

"You know them," she said. "I told you ... earlier."

"So you did, so you did," he agreed. "As I recall them you seem to agree with Hector in blackguarding me. I was an unnatural father to get rid of an unwanted burden by foisting her on his own son. It's as well m'back's broad."

"I didn't say that," said Elizabeth indignantly.

"That's precisely what you meant. Now, I may be all you both say I am, but I'm not in m'dotage yet and there's one thing stands out as plain as the nose on m'face. Neither of you objects to the other."

There was a short and embarrassed silence.

"You could hardly expect Elizabeth to voice such objections to my face," said Hector harshly.

"There was nothing to stop her voicing them to me, and you should have heard what she called me! Haven't you realized that Liz isn't exactly a bread-and-butter miss?"

Hector smiled appreciatively.

"I know, but even so ..."

"I give my word, both of you, if this match is not

62

agreeable, we'll find another way out of the wood. But I'm convinced it's a solution which'll suit you both now and later. Hector, you get a wife who might have been bred to be the wife of a diplomat, clever as paint, a linguist who can put most of the so-called interpreters in the legations to shame and accustomed since she was a child to housekeeping in foreign cities. And Liz gets ... what was it you wanted, girl ... rational employment, wasn't it? It won't be a sinecure bein' married to Hector. And it solves all our immediate problems. And while we're speakin' plainly I may as well tell the pair of you I've had this match in my eye this past six months."

They both looked up at him, startled.

"Didn't mean to do it this way. Thought I'd take Liz to Paris in the spring for a visit, y'know the sort of thing. As it is, well, it's sudden, and it's come sooner than I'd looked for, but to my mind it's still a good notion."

He hauled a massive watch out of his fob.

"I'm due at Queen's Gardens in half an hour. Goin' to persuade Cousin Amelia to leave her brood for a day or two. Must have some kind of a chaperone for Liz. Goin' to be enough talk as it is. Well, what d'ye say?"

Elizabeth looked up and caught a glimpse of the amusement in Hector's eyes. It was too much for her and she began to laugh. Lacombe smiled paternally upon them.

"Good. Now, we'll have no more of your fiddle-faddlin' objections. Sensible pair. Talk it over."

He departed and could be heard shouting for Baker in the hall. Elizabeth felt the laughter die in her and walked over to the window.

"Old fox!" said Hector, with affection, "but I won't have you feel he's got you cornered, Liz. You've only to say, but you must know that."

Elizabeth didn't answer at once. Hector joined her at the window, and she turned to face him.

"I must be honest about this, Hector. How will Madame de Mavanne feel when she hears of this? Will she not be hurt?"

"I don't believe she will."

Hector spoke slowly.

"It isn't easy to explain. This isn't a ... grand passion, Liz, not for either of us. It was a sudden impulse, because it was summer, because she was happy for the first time in months, because I was so *damnably* sorry for her. And she is, well, pretty, like one of those wax dolls you see in the toy-shop. But I regret what happened because it meant so little to me and she ... she was almost desperate with remorse. I did explain that she is very devout?"

Elizabeth nodded.

"I don't think," he went on, "that I am deceiving myself when I tell you that I think she will welcome the news of my marriage."

"How can you say that?" exclaimed Elizabeth, "She may be ... she might ... you cannot be sure ..."

"I think she is fond of me, grateful for what little I have done for her. But, I have the feeling that each time she sees me I remind her that she has sinned. It is an uncomfortable feeling. She might welcome the news for another reason. If it became necessary, and it may, we could provide a home for the child."

He said this quietly, his eyes on her face as she looked into the square outside. She glanced at him, puzzled.

"Of course we could. But why may it be necessary?"

Hector smiled slightly.

"You vindicate my father's taste, Liz. I assure you, such

64

a proposition would not be acceptable to most of the women I know."

Elizabeth went pink.

"You knew already how lacking in delicacy I was."

He laughed.

"Poor Cousin Froggie. Imagine his chagrin when he sees his paper tomorrow. Won't that reconcile you to the prospect?"

"It certainly helps," she agreed with a chuckle.

"Does that dispose of your main fiddle-faddling objection?"

"It wasn't an objection, it was a qualm. You see, I must be honest, nothing else will do ... I don't really need to be reconciled to the prospect. It's as if someone had opened a door for me."

She looked straight at him.

"To my mind it is you who have the thin end of the bargain."

He smiled.

"Believe me, Liz, I am content enough. Indeed the better we become acquainted the more I think that I am luckier than I deserve."

"You are very kind to say so."

He held out his hand.

"I promise you one thing, Liz, I will try never to be less than kind."

She put her hand in his.

"I don't know what I should promise. To be what you need as far as I can. Will that do?"

"Indeed it will."

He raised her hand to his lips and kissed it lightly.

"There is one other matter," he said, holding on to her hand and looking at it as if he had never seen one before, "I ... you said last night that you had always wanted a

E

brother. I'll be that brother ... unless you ... until you ... do you understand me?"

"You are more than considerate," said Elizabeth gravely, "but I would not like ... there is the question of the succession."

"There is time enough to be thinking of that," he replied, "besides, that wily old badger shows every sign of outliving the pair of us. Now, run and put on your bonnet. I am going to take you to Rundell's and buy you a ruby. I hope you like rubies?"

"I do."

"Good, because I think they will become you."

Elizabeth turned back into the room and caught sight of the clock on the chimney-piece. The sight of it seemed to amuse her.

"You realise, don't you, that this time yesterday we hadn't even seen one another?" she exclaimed.

"I do remember remarking shortly after we did meet that our acquaintance seemed to be ripening with remarkable speed!"

"But I doubt if even you realised just how fast."

When she got to the door she turned suddenly and found him close behind her. They both spoke together.

"You are perfectly ..."

"Liz, you are cer ..."

They both laughed at one another and he gave her a quick brotherly hug.

"Run along. No more fiddle-faddling."

"I seem to detect," she observed drily, "a distinct family likeness."

Cousin Amelia was a motherly creature with a romantic soul. She abandoned her large family to their assortment of nursemaids, governesses, and tutors for the coming week

66

and threw herself into wedding preparations with enjoyment, saying with a certain monotonous regularity that it would get her into practice for her own daughters. An hour before she arrived in a flurry of dress-baskets, Aunt Frobisher had departed for the station in a procession of well-laden four-wheelers, escorted by her son who seemed less than pleased at finding that his mother was now to be a charge upon him rather than his uncle. He could be heard remonstrating with her on the steps, but she would not listen. The information contained in the papers the following morning was conveyed to her by James, for once speechless. It provoked her into writing a long letter to her brother which was a curious mixture of indignation and olive-branch. It arrived on the morning of the wedding. He read it, snorted with amusement and dropped it in the fire.

"Yer aunt's in a pickle," he announced to Hector who was conferring with the much-tried Enderby in the corner, "she'd apologise if she knew how, but she's not sure what to apologise for or whether it's worth the try."

"I feel sure your withers are unwrung."

"Lord, yes. All the same ... Enderby, remind me to send her a draft on m'bank. Couple o' ponies."

"Yes, sir."

"Conscience money?" enquired his son undutifully.

"Cheap at the price," replied his father obscurely, "the roof's leakin'. Not her fault."

Baker interrupted them.

"A letter sent round by hand for Mr. Hector, sir."

Hector ripped it open and read the few lines it contained.

"We'll have to leave for Paris tonight. I'm to go to St. Petersburg."

"Posted?" asked his father sharply.

"No. For a month or so only. It's because I've been

working on this affair of the capitulations and the Holy Places. Normanby seems to think I might be able to help arrange some sort of compromise on this affair."

. Lacombe nodded.

"Don't see us dippin' in the same dish with Czar Nicholas, whatever Pam hopes. French won't like it either. They want to keep in with Johnny Turk and keep the Holy Places in the hands of the Catholics."

"So you think we'll go on propping up the Porte?"

"It's that or have the Cossacks in the Balkans," said his father bluntly, "and that's too near Egypt for comfort. There's the India trade to consider. Mind you, if Pam can put off a clash over the Holy Land for a while, so much the better. It's a choice of evils, m'boy, a choice of evils. A pity you'll have to leave Liz so soon."

"It won't be for long."

"If you think that, m'boy, you've never had much to do with the Russians. They're worse than the Spaniards. Time you and Enderby were off to the church. I'll break the news to Liz."

He bustled them out of the house and made his way upstairs to Elizabeth's room. Cousin Amelia had departed for the church ten minutes before in a flutter of feathered bonnet and smelling-bottles. Catriona came out as he knocked on the door, her eyes red and her new wedding bonnet on one side. She bobbed at him and scuttled downstairs sniffing.

"Can I come in, m'dear?"

"Of course. I'm quite ready."

Elizabeth was standing by the window looking out.

"What's upset Whatsername?"

She smiled.

"Oh, Catriona. She'd a notion of Brussels lace and a church crammed with guests and a prince of the blood waiting at the altar. She's a silly creature in some ways."

Lacombe joined her at the window.

"And what about your notions, m'dear?"

Elizabeth looked gravely at him.

"Do you mean that a wedding like this is not ... not what I dreamed about?"

"Something of the kind."

"I didn't dream about weddings."

"What then?"

"I hoped I might meet someone who would treat me as Father did, as you do, as a person, not a household pet-dog, of being allowed to ... to be more than just a brood-mare or a table ornament."

She smiled.

"So you see why I am not weeping. The only thing is, I wish I could be sure ..."

"Don't you fret about Hector, m'girl. He'll do. And he knows it. He's a lucky man."

"I'll do my best for him," said Liz.

His Lordship patted her on the shoulder.

"No need to tell me that."

Liz began to gather her gloves and the posy of flowers which she was to carry.

"'Nother thing," said Lacombe suddenly, "ye've heard me talk of the boy's mother. Good sweet girl. Boy's like her, not me. Good thing. Hadn't spoken to her above twice in m'life when we got married. M'parents arranged it. I was in Vienna and m'father far gone. Wanted to see me settled before he·snuffed it."

His face hardened.

"Her parents pushed her into it. I was quite a *parti*, y'know, with the title and the money, and they'd not a sixpence and three others to settle. She was so frightened she could hardly speak. But I'll tell you a thing, Liz. At the end of two days I knew we'd go along well enough, and we did. Happy as crickets. Till she died. She got the child-bed fever when our second was born. They both died. I miss her yet and it must be twenty-five years. Don't say there hasn't been a woman here and there, but I keep thinking, I must tell her this an' that, an' then rememberin' she's dead, even after all these years."

He cleared his throat and glared at her.

"What I mean to say's this: you've as good a chance to make a match of it as anyone. Better in fact. No damned airy notions about each other."

Liz kissed him on the cheek.

"Now, we'd best get along. I've a thing to tell you before we get to church. Hector's had a note from the Office sent round this morning ..."

5

Elizabeth to Hector.   Paris. December 1850.

... by now I feel as if I had been living in Paris for years rather than weeks. Your house has been arranged to my satisfaction. I have left a good deal for you to decide when you return and some rooms are shut up at present as I am not entertaining to any great degree.

You are to have a refuge on the ground floor and I have had glass doors put in so that you may escape from unwelcome callers (and importunate wives) into a charming garden. Your books are all arranged. Catriona set them on the shelves in order of size which resulted in some strange bedfellows, but I have since shelved them in a less arbitrary manner. I have also visited the Paris bookshops and added a few ...

Catriona has made some headway with the French tongue mainly to be able to castigate the French girls in an appropriate manner. But even the Gaelic cannot do justice to her opinion of the French people. However, her memories of the Dover packet are still vivid and she has confided to me that even permanent residence in this "heathen, dirty and forsaken country" would be preferable to another Channel crossing. It is hard to see Catriona as the daughter of generations of fisher-folk ... like myself.

You might think from the foregoing that I am confined wholly to the house and the company of the servants, but this is not the case at all. Your friends have been overwhelming in their attentions and no day has passed without its meed of callers and invitations. Madame de Villette has been kind enough to chaperone me to many houses and we have become great friends. I take much delight in her tongue which is well-salted and I have heard every Paris scandal since Waterloo. As you suggested, I told her (in the strictest confidence) of our "long-standing attachment" and I have to report that it was mentioned the other day by a complete stranger as a "touching romance". However, she considers that I live too retired (and I haven't dined alone since you left!) and laments my lack of a manservant. I told her that I intended to wait for your return before engaging one but my real reason is that Catriona has no opinion of them at all and I want a quiet life ...

Hector to Elizabeth   St. Petersburg. January 1851.
... I now realise that I might be here for some months which is not a pleasing prospect. News is very slow to arrive and I am more grateful than I can say for your long informative letters which keep me in touch with affairs in Paris. May I congratulate you upon the precis you prepare for me. My father must be regretting your absence. That fox-hunting young blockhead he calls a secretary is not a circumstance to you.

It is exceedingly cold, cold enough for this statement not to be a mere pleasantry. I am most thankful that I am unlikely to appear to you as a *doppelganger*, not that you would recognise this fur-wrapped, perambulating heap of clothing. I resemble nothing so much as a bear. By the same token I am not the sole inhabitant of these necessary furs. I dispute their possession with a legion of the largest and most aggressive fleas I ever encountered. No effort of mine or my man's will serve to evict them. If you have a remedy I implore you to send it. The Russian appears to regard them as an inescapable part of existence.

I have no very good news from the Rue des Saintes, the widow Leroux tells me that her mistress is far from well. I appreciate very much your offer to go and visit there and I wish it was possible. However, as things are, it might be unwise. The wretched husband is in Paris and, so I am informed, still very much on the *qui vive*. They have your direction should the need arise, and I hope and pray it may not.

I am inclined to agree with Mme. de Villette on the question of a manservant. From what you tell me Paris is restive just now and I would feel happier to think you had some protection other than a pack of women, however devoted ...

Elizabeth to Hector.   Paris. January 1851.
... there is much talk of a "second empire" these days, and there can be little doubt that Louis-Napoleon is intending to try to make his Presidency into something more permanent. His adherents are bobbing up in various strategic posts and the Assembly is too divided to make any concerted opposition. At our Embassy there have been indignant whispers about the possibility of a Bonapartist coup. No need to tell me of Lord Normanby's leaning to the Orleanists for his Embassy is haunted by Royalists, ineffective creatures on the whole, except for one Pierre de Mavanne. I would dislike that man even if I did not know how he has treated Eloise. Your father's letters are indiscreet to say the least. He is

vitriolic about the Queen and her husband (thinly disguised as Herr and Frau Albert) because they will interfere with his beloved Pam. He seems to think that this situation may be pushed to a crisis before long and tells me he doesn't trust Johnnie Russell an inch.

I enclose a report of yesterday's proceedings in the Assembly. They may be of interest and to my unregenerate eye are funnier than any Sketch by Boz.

You and Madame de Villette have your way and the establishment is increased by a veritable personage. He arrived three days ago with a letter from Mme. de Villette. She was anxious, she told me, to find Jacques a worthy place, and hoped in this way to do well by both of us. With this letter he sent up a bundle of what I can only describe as eulogia. He appears to have spent what time he has not spent with royalty in serving practically every notable figure in Paris. I sent for him to come up and waited for this paragon with bated breath. He was something less impressive than his testimonials. If you resemble a bear he is like nothing so much as a plump monkey. I can see him perched upon an organ-grinder's barrow without the slightest difficulty. But he has vast assurance. He assured me in the first few minutes that already there were a number of households clamouring for his services (Madame too had told me this) but despite his youthful appearance he was no longer young and had decided that it was time for him to abandon the larger establishments and exercise his talents in a more restricted field. He assured me (among a variety of other things) that it was unthinkable that we could continue without his services for another day and he proposed to enter upon his duties immediately by dismissing the unsuitable young person who had admitted him. As I had already come to the

same conclusion about the girl in question it was difficult to deny the necessity of this and having agreed to
the change I found that in some mysterious manner we
had entered upon a period of a month's probation on
either side. He unbent at this point and assured me that
I would wonder how ever I had managed without him.

After three days I am inclined to believe him. He has
mended every faulty item in the house, from the flue
in the kitchen to the handle of my wardrobe. He has
opened the small saloon to be used as dining room
when we are *en famille* because he disapproved of the
distance between the kitchen and the dining saloon.
He has completely renewed and improved the system
of bells throughout the house. At this moment I can see
him in the garden tying up a shrub which was blown
down by last night's gale. Anything less like one's usual
notion of a butler would be hard to find. I have one tiny
cloud, no larger than a man's hand at present. Catriona
has so far refused to discuss the appointment with me
at all and has indeed been treating me with an icy
reserve which is her usual prelude to a scene which will
shake the rafters. To make matters worse Jacques has
cast a penetrating eye on Catriona's mentor, Yvette, and
has hinted that she is pilfering from the kitchen. *Absit
omen* and *caelum ruat.*

You will be relieved to hear, after such an account,
that our cook is a lifelong friend of his and that he
much commends your perspicacity in engaging him. He
was also kind enough to commend my taste for white
paint and muslin curtains but considers that we require
some pictures for the hall and stairway. Before he could
recommend the painters and commission the pictures
I explained that this was one of the things which I intended to leave until you returned. He assured me that

I was perfectly justified in such a decision as you were a well-known amateur of art. Are you, my dear? There is such a lot I do not know about you.

He is not really such a grotesque as may appear from this letter. He is in truth very competent and conversant with all his more conventional duties. He has an uncanny gift for anticipating one's wishes which argues a genuine kindness, a quality I value. Moreover, he knows everyone in Paris who is anyone and I find this uncommonly useful in gathering news for you. But I do wish he had not set Catriona all upon end ...

Hector to Elizabeth. February 1851.

... how I abominate these endless delays and procrastinations. I can see no end to these discussions and (between ourselves) no possible outcome. Besides I am weary beyond expression of cold, snow, vast, interminable, ill-served meals and vodka ... how I detest the stuff. I go about very little because there is much distress and unrest in the city. Want has given rise to disease and I have been told not to risk infection of the Embassy staff. Everything seems to be black or white and it is a good six weeks yet before we can expect any signs of spring.

What a boon your letters have been these past weary weeks. I have read and re-read them till I can almost say them by heart. Without your news and your accounts of a more civilised existence I must have fallen into a melancholy. You have a gift, Liz, for the writing of letters. You say there is such a lot you do not know about me but whether you know it or not you have told me so much about yourself that when I return I will feel as if I am coming back to an old friend rather than a new wife. On reflection I might have expressed that more happily but I trust you will accept the spirit of appreciation in which it was written. I look forward more than I can say to coming home to you ...

Elizabeth to Hector.   February 1851.
... I did tell you, did I not, that your Aunt Frobisher wrote me an olive branch at Christmas in which she forgave me ... for what, I am not entirely certain, and I do not think that she is ... and gave us her blessing in four crossed pages which took me some time to decipher. The meat of the matter was in the postscript in which she told me, not without a distinct note of triumph, that James was married some three weeks after we left England. As it chanced I knew, for your father had told me in two searing lines. The fortunate female was a Miss Roper. Aunt describes her as, "a very good sort of girl" and your father as, "a perfect fright but very comfortably circumstanced". I hardly know what to expect, yes expect. James writes by yesterday's post to tell me that he and his dear Joanna intend to make a wedding-tour in the spring and hope to come to Paris. I must admit to the basest curiosity to see her.

The crocuses are out so spring has begun its long journey north to you. Would it be forward in me to say I wish I could come with it ...

Hector to Elizabeth.   March 1851.
... I am doomed never to have cheerful intelligence. The Russians appear determined on meddling in the east no matter what representations we make and my great hope is that Pam may at last see the folly of making these representations and I may be released from durance vile. Like you I am curious to see Mrs. James. Cousin Froggie must have a-wooing gone with

indecent haste. Not, now I come to think on it, that we have any room to speak on such a subject. It is almost incredible to me now that we have met for less than three days. I feel as if you had been a part of my existence all my life.

The news from the Rue des Saintes is distressing. The good widow included a note from the doctor in her last letter. He seems to be a pleasant, competent young man. He tells me that both her lungs are affected and that he cannot be sanguine about her condition. The birth is expected early in May if all goes well. I wish I could be sure I will be back by then ...

Elizabeth to Hector.   March 1851.

... I am most distressed by what you tell me. I wish there were something I could do, but it seems I am forced to add to your worries. I would not send you this if I didn't feel sure that it was something you ought to know. The enclosed is a cutting from *Le Parisien* of last week:

"We have much regret in announcing the death of Madame Eloise de la Rivière. Her aimiable eccentricities and lively tongue were a source of much pleasure to her intimates and she will be much missed. Her whole fortune, a considerable amount for she died childless, is bequeathed to her brother's daughter, Madame de Mavanne, whose disappearance from society in the summer of last year gave rise to much speculation. It seems possible that the search for her will be earnestly conducted."

I would have sent you this in any event but an odd occurrence on the day after it appeared has made me uneasy. I ride daily, as I told you, and on this occasion it was wet and cold so I came home early, entering the house by the glass doors into your study. I must confess to using this apartment more than I should: you may have a task to evict me on your return. I found the parlour maid carefully examining all the papers on the desk and in the drawers which I had left unlocked. I dismissed her at once and told Jacques to enquire very nearly into the background of anyone he engages to replace her. The girl swore that she was merely wanting to find a stray coin because her family is in distress and that she cannot read. Jacques assures me that he finds upon enquiry that she was an orphan and was educated by the nuns.

I am as sure as I can be that she could have found nothing to interest anyone. I have your letters locked away safely in quite another place ...

Hector to Elizabeth.   March 1851.
... you were quite right to be uneasy. There is almost certainly some connection between the two events. I beg you, take the greatest care. Burn my letters as soon as you have read them. I enclose a letter from Eloise. I know this is a strange thing for a man to send his wife but I am confident that you will not take it amiss and it will explain better than ever I could why it is so important to be careful that no hint of her whereabouts should leak out. It drives me almost distracted to be tied here by the heel at such a time. I have written to my father in the hope that he can do something to release me ...

Eloise to Hector.   March 1851.
... Dr. Massin is always reassuring but I know I haven't long. I am sorry if you are distressed but for myself I am almost glad. All that concerns me is the child,

if it should survive me. My husband *must not* have it. I depend on you, my good friend, to prevent this. My aunt's legacy will keep it in comfort and this relieves my mind. I have claimed the money through a lawyer friend of Dr. Massin and made my will. The doctor and the lawyer are to be trustees. You are not named though they both know what I want you to do. This will be best, for legally the child can be regarded as my husband's if he chooses to acknowledge it. He would acknowledge an imp of the pit to get his hands on half the sum.

Make what arrangements you wish for the child. I trust you to do what is best. Goodbye, dear friend, and thank you for your great kindness to me ...

Elizabeth to Hector.   April 1851.
... a hint to Jacques was enough. The house has become a discreet fortress and he has taken the blame, if that is the word, upon his shoulders, pretending to have an abiding fear of robbers. I have disobeyed you in the matter of your letters. Forgive me, but I did not wish to burn them. Believe me when I say that they, and the note from Eloise which I could hardly bear to read, are perfectly safe.

There is great indignation here over the Russian gestures in the East. All talk at such gatherings as I attend revolves around the various treaties and capitulations and the rights and privileges of the Latins over the custody of the Holy Places. Am I being uncommonly insensitive to find it all somehow hollow? Nevertheless I will welcome all the brouhaha if, as I believe, it may be a portent of your return. It is obvious, even to me, that our relations with Russia are not improving. I have another portent in the shape of a note from your father.

He is obviously busy for young Enderby wrote it. It is
odd to see your father's trenchancies (is there such a
word?) written in the hand of a schoolboy. He tells me
he intends to visit us, not me, US in the early summer.
I take this as a good omen if not something more.
Would he have written to announce a visit as early
as this? More like him to descend upon us un-
heralded ...

F

6

"And I am telling you we did very well before he came!" said Catriona. "It is putting me out of my room he is now, without a by-your-leave!"

"He did ask your leave, and mine too," Elizabeth attempted to stem the flood, "and it is a much pleasanter room."

"I was happy enough where I was," stormed Catriona. "I am not wanting another room. It was fine and handy, so it was."

"Well you needn't go, if you don't want to," said Elizabeth, "it was just that ..."

"I know fine what it was, it was just interfering, that's what it was. He must aye be at something: if it's not one thing it's another. I would like fine to know who it is owns this house, you or that ..."

Catriona rattled out a comprehensive Gaelic epithet which startled Elizabeth.

"Catriona!" she exclaimed in the same tongue, "Take care what you are saying!"

Catriona folded her lips into a hard line and stood her ground.

"I have been with you, mo chridhe, since you were no bigger than this my arm. Am I to be told daily what is best for you by a man not in the house ten minutes and him a foreigner? He is one must have his own way no matter what, and I am not to be made a nothing under your roof. And I am telling to you there is no room for the both of the two of us under it."

She stalked off to the door.

"Be a little tolerant," begged Elizabeth. "Do I not need you both? If I have a word with him ..."

"It is many, many words you will be needing," returned Catriona, "if you are to stop his mouth. And more words yet if you are to stop me going home to my father's house."

She vanished, slamming the door behind her, and Elizabeth sat a moment in thought before she sighed, and rang for Jacques.

"Jacques, do you know what I want to say to you? It would be most unlike you if you didn't."

"It is, without doubt, concerning the good Catriona," he announced. "It is a woman of decided temperament, that one."

"I'm extremely glad you appreciate that, Jacques, because somehow you must learn to adapt to this ... temperament."

He made a complicated gesture of assent.

"But of course, Madame, this goes without saying, without saying. The good Catriona, she is your nurse and she is of a devotion to yourself which moves me extremely, I assure you. If it must come to a choice, what would you? I can without difficulty find another post. *I* will not starve, me."

"But, Jacques, you are a person of such address," pleaded Elizabeth, "surely it needn't come to this?"

Jacques shrugged.

"As for me I am content here. It is what I like, a small

household, little ceremony and cultured. No, Madame, I have no wish to leave your service."

He coughed.

"This situation, I have seen it developing. And I have a plan."

He hesitated for a second and glanced at Elizabeth somewhat slyly.

"It would entail a certain small and forgivable deception and Madame would need to aid me."

"Go on," said Elizabeth.

"This ... this commotion, it comes of jealousy," explained Jacques, "in the circumstances I am useful to you as she cannot be. You are kind to me, laugh at me as you do at her and tolerate my long tongue."

He twinkled a smile at her.

"I have not been in service for more than thirty years and not to have been told of my faults! The good Catriona, she thinks I am taking her place in your regard ... bear with me yet a moment ... and because of this she detests me. Nothing I can do is right. Now what you and I must do, Madame, is to have a dispute, to fight, you understand me?"

"Fight!"

"Perfectly, Madame. You must perceive that it is necessary. You will fly out upon me on some matter which I will contrive, something of little consequence. You will be angry and declare that I must go and go at once. I will fly to the good Catriona and weep a little and lament my grey hairs and the difficulty in finding suitable employment at my age and protest my devotion to yourself and beg that she will intercede with you on my behalf, to prevent my being turned off without a character."

"It would never work," said Elizabeth. "Without wish-

84

ing to wound you, Jacques, I think she would welcome the news."

"Madame cannot have considered. This Catriona, she has a heart as big as Notre Dame," said Jacques with a wave of his hand. "Moreover, you are her nursling, it would reflect upon her that you are unjust and unkind. This she will not permit. And for me in my distress she will have pity and forget her dislike."

"Well . . ."

"It will serve for the moment, Madame. For the future I have other plans."

"Indeed."

"Yes, but I will not trouble Madame with them for the present," continued Jacques airily. "As Madame has observed herself, I am not without address and much of my life has been spent attempting to anticipate the vagaries of females."

"Forgive the personal nature of this question, Jacques, but have you ever been married?"

"Yes, Madame, but she is dead these many years and with the angels."

He paused for a thoughtful moment.

"And it would take the blessed angels to deal with her," he added, twinkling, "for she was not unlike the good Catriona. But enough of this. Tomorrow, Madame, something will occur."

"What, Jacques?"

"As to that I do not yet know, but I will contrive something. You will send for me and berate me heartily and tell me to go. I will see to it that she is in earshot of this little comedy. Thereafter leave it to me. All will come about as I say."

85

"We will have to be really clever to convince her. She is no fool."

Jacques bowed.

"Of this I am aware.. But neither are we, Madame, neither are we."

On this optimistic note he departed leaving Elizabeth with an overwhelming desire to share her amusement ... and her apprehension of the part she would have to play. She sat down at her desk and had just launched into a description of the two interviews for Hector's benefit when Catriona bustled in with a note in her hand which she regarded as if it might bite her.

"A boy was just bringing this," she announced. "He said it was very important and then he ran off as if the devil was after him."

The note was not long.

Chère Madame,

The baby has come and is a fine girl and healthy but the poor mother is sinking. M'sieur told me to send for you if this happened and that you would care for the child. Monsieur the Doctor says that there is not much time and my mistress wishes very much to see you. Please come at once.

Angélique Leroux.

Elizabeth frowned, put the note into her desk and locked it up.

"Send Jacques to me, Catriona, please," she said.

"What can you be wanting with that one?" Catriona protested angrily.

"Oh, hold your peace! This is more important than any of your squabbles," snapped Elizabeth. "I have work for you too. Prepare the little back bedchamber and the dressing room beside it. I will be bringing back a baby when I return."

Catriona gasped.

"Dhia! A baby! Whose? How old?"

"Newborn. Take Régine and buy what will be needed . . . a crib, blankets, clothes, you'll know better than I."

"Who better, indeed! But what . . ."

"Never mind that, and mind, Catriona, go to shops where you are not known. Don't talk about this outside the house, and see that Régine does not either. It's important. I'll explain when I have time. Now, ask Jacques to come to me."

Catriona departed on this distasteful errand with no more than a sniff and Jacques appeared within a few minutes.

"I have a task to try even your capacity, Jacques. I want you to find a good wet-nurse by tonight."

Jacques bowed, his face expressionless.

"Yes, Madame, a wet-nurse."

"She must be young, healthy and, well, suitable."

"I understand perfectly, Madame."

"I am going out now and when I come back I will have a baby with me. Catriona has gone to prepare the rooms. Ask Fernand to call me a cab. I want to go to Notre Dame."

"Will Madame not take the carriage," protested Jacques, "it will be warmer, cleaner . . ."

"No. I'll take a hack. And at once."

"Of course, Madame."

"And Jacques . . ."

"Madame?"

"I don't want a single word of this to leak out. No one in the household must mention a word outside. Not one word, or they will be looking for another situation."

For the first time since he had come in Jacques' expression altered.

"Madame!" he protested, "the rest is possible but that will require a holy miracle."

Elizabeth got up from her desk.

"In that case, Jacques, you will have to pray very hard for it is extremely important. Use threats, bribes, tell them any story which seems good to you, but they must not talk."

Jacques cast his eyes up to heaven and withdrew. Elizabeth running upstairs for a heavy cloak and her largest bonnet chuckled to herself at the memory of his expression.

Elizabeth dismissed the cab outside Notre Dame and among the labyrinth of narrow streets nearby found a shop which sold what she was looking for. She bought a heavy, black widow's veil and an equally sombre woollen shawl. These she put on in the shop under the incurious gaze of the old woman who had sold them to her. There was a cab-rank in the square and in a few minutes she was on her way to the Rue des Saintes.

The street lay in a quiet district of tall, narrow-fronted, grey stone houses which were now divided into apartments. The driver stopped outside number seven and she paid him off, waiting until he was out of sight before she crossed the road to number ten. Inside the heavy front door, the concierge's loge was open and a sallow-faced woman peered out at her.

"You are expected, Madame, be pleased to ascend at once. It is upon the first floor."

The staircase was ill-lit but the first floor landing was flooded with light which came through the open door of the apartment. A dumpy little woman dressed in black bombazine, her face pink and swollen with crying, was waiting for her.

"Madame Leroux?" enquired Elizabeth.

The little creature nodded and held the door for her to pass. From somewhere in the apartment came the thin cry of a new-born baby.

"M'sieu the doctor is with her," said Madame Leroux, ushering Elizabeth into a bedchamber, "and he asks you to have the goodness to wait a few moments for him. We have made the salon into a sickroom, you understand, it was more cheerful than this room and I could hear her more easily when . . ."

The tears welled up again and Madame Leroux dabbed at her face with a damp scrap of linen. Elizabeth moved over to the crib which was set near the fireplace and removed her black veil with relief.

"And here is the baby," she said.

"Yes, Madame, poor mite, poor, poor little creature. She has much to lament."

Madame Leroux picked up the shawl-wrapped bundle and cuddled it till the wails subsided.

"What is she to be called?"

The question provoked a fresh outburst of weeping.

"She will not see her," sobbed Madame, "she will not talk of her. She waits for you to choose a name. She has said this."

Elizabeth took the child while the unhappy woman tried ineffectively to dry her eyes. The baby seemed incredibly tiny and fragile and perfect, the unfocussed blue eyes fringed with long, dark wet lashes. Elizabeth felt an icy stirring in her stomach at the realization that she would from now on be responsible for this frail scrap. The blue eyes closed and the baby slept, undisturbed by Madame's sobs. At this point the door opened and a lanky figure

89

entered. He was young, not more than thirty, and so thin that Elizabeth's first reaction to his appearance was to wonder when he had last had a square meal. He was in shirtsleeves and upon the right one was a stain of new blood. He saw Madame's eye upon it and rolled the sleeve up above his elbow.

"Madame l'Anglaise has come," muttered the widow. "This is Doctor Massin, Madame. He has been so good, so attentive, one cannot conceive ..."

Dr. Massin reddened a little at this encomium and nodded to Elizabeth.

"You are to take *la p'tite,* Madame, I understand," he remarked and moved over to peer into the baby's face, "she is a fine healthy child. And it would seem she has taken to you. This is excellent."

He smiled at her and this transformed the rather saturnine face.

"And the mother?" enquired Elizabeth.

The smile vanished.

"She is very weak. It is a question of an hour or two at most. Since we sent for you she has had another haemorrhage."

He took the baby gently from Elizabeth and replaced her in the crib. She did not waken.

"Madame de Mavanne is very anxious to speak to you," he said, "but she refuses even to look at her baby."

"I think I can understand that," said Elizabeth.

"Do you indeed?"

He looked at her intently for a moment.

"She is conscious at the moment," he said at last, "and you can come in now if you will, but you must realize that she is dying. It is not an easy death, Madame. You understand me?"

Elizabeth nodded. His voice was harsh.

"Reassure her about *la p'tite,*" he said more gently, "I am sure you can. That will give her more relief at this stage than anything I can do."

He paused and frowned as if he was taking a difficult decision and then turned to Madame Leroux.

"Is there a priest nearby, Madame? It is high time to send for him."

7

Madame Leroux scuttled out of the room, sniffing unhappily. Elizabeth waited for the doctor to take her in to Eloise but instead he went to a desk which stood on the dressing chest, unlocked it and took out a bundle of papers. These he handed to Elizabeth.

"She asked me to give you these to return to your husband. They are his letters. She said to tell you to read them."

Elizabeth looked up in surprise and found him smiling at her.

"They are good letters. I have seen them. Kind and cheerful, but not those of a lover. She wants you to know this, to understand what it was between them. Not to resent it."

"I don't resent it," said Elizabeth, rather shakily, for she was moved by this gesture, "I have no right to resent it. And would I be here if I did?"

"You'll forgive me if I say that Eloise is not thinking of you so much as of the child. She does not want you to resent her."

Elizabeth glanced across at the crib.

"As if I could."

The doctor shrugged.

"Time passes and people change," he observed, "and, doubtless you will have children of your own."

He turned back to the desk before she could reply to this.

"My friend, Maître Leblanc, has told me to give you this. It's a copy of her will. Trust him but don't approach him directly. This might be dangerous. He has made arrangements to look after the child's affairs and would like to have the name of your man of business in England."

He watched Elizabeth place the papers safely in her reticule and frowned.

"There is one thing more ..."

He paused and seemed to have some difficulty in going on.

"I ... I have come to have a regard for Eloise, and perhaps she has a little for me. I am not a believer. To me the child is all that will be left of her."

He was jerking out the words with difficulty.

"If she had lived, who knows? But there was never any chance of that. She must have been consumptive for years."

There was a pause.

"She had been starving for two months before your husband found her. Did he tell you that?"

Elizabeth shook her head.

"Her mother and both her sisters died of the same disease," he said sombrely, "there was little hope for her even then. He is not to think he killed her. He did not. If anything he gave her a reprieve, an interlude of peace and comfort. And he let her die in comfort. Tell him this. It is true and it may help him accept the child."

He pulled at the collar of his shirt and produced a gold coin strung from a chain.

"Keep this for *la p'tite*. It is a luck-piece. I'd like her to have it. Tell her about me some day and say ... oh, say I wish I had been her father."

93

Without surprise Elizabeth saw that there were tears in his dark eyes. She said nothing but wrapped the token carefully in her handkerchief and stowed it away.

"She was all her father had left," he exclaimed savagely, "so he sold her to de Mavanne for a paltry political advantage. De Mavanne who was three times her age and had killed two wives already."

"M'sieu!" protested Elizabeth faintly.

"Oh, he didn't murder them," said the doctor, "nothing so merciful ..."

He stopped short and regained control of himself.

"Come," he said briskly, "if you are to see her before the priest arrives we had best go in now."

They went into the tiny vestibule and he led the way into the sickroom. At the door he paused and spoke very quietly.

"What distresses me so much ... she is afraid, horribly afraid. She has sinned and she feels guilty. I cannot comfort her, she knows I am not a believer."

They went in. There was a nun of a nursing order by the bedside who left the room at the doctor's nod.

"... she was pretty ... like one of those wax dolls you see in the toy-shops." As Elizabeth stood by the bed she could hear Hector's voice saying those words. Almost nothing of this prettiness was left now. The pink and white skin was greyish-yellow, the huge blue eyes faded and ringed with purple shadows. The claw-like hands moved restlessly on the sheet.

As soon as they came close to the bed Eloise turned her head towards Elizabeth and looked at her hard.

"You are Elizabeth?"

Her voice was weak and hoarse. Elizabeth nodded and moved to stand beside her. The room smelt of drugs and stale air and blood.

"I had to see you," said Eloise, "you do not mind?"

"I would have come before this," replied Elizabeth calmly.

"I know. Hector told me."

Dr. Massin began to count Eloise's pulse. She took no notice but continued to stare at Elizabeth. After nearly a minute she seemed satisfied with what she saw.

"You will take my baby?"

"I will," said Elizabeth. "She'll be like my own. I promise you."

"It's very well."

Eloise closed her eyes. When she spoke again her voice was weaker.

"She should have an English name," she muttered, "you must choose it for she will be yours."

Elizabeth glanced at Dr. Massin who nodded. She sat down on the bed and took one of the terrible hands in her own, it felt dry and burning hot.

"How would you like 'Louisa'?"

The colourless lips moved into a faint smile.

"Louisa. Yes. That is English and yet ..."

"That is what I thought."

"It's a strange meeting this," said Eloise after a long pause. "I wish we could have met before. We could have been friends, I believe."

"I would have liked that."

There was a brief silence and then the hot fingers tightened their grip on Elizabeth's hand.

"Edouard has told you? My husband, he must not have the child. He is a devil, cruel, I could not rest ..."

"Well, you may be easy, my friend," said Elizabeth calmly, "we won't let him have her. I give you my word."

The feeble grip relaxed and the eyes closed again.

"She will be safe in England ... cool and green ... I went once, long ago ..."

The weak voice faded and after a few moments Elizabeth began to think that Eloise was unconscious or asleep, but just then she began to move restlessly. Dr. Massin watched her, his face expressionless.

"I sin, others must pay for it," muttered the dying woman, "I am wicked, wicked. God will punish me ..."

The doctor looked at Elizabeth and jerked his chin towards the door. She rose obediently but Eloise had felt her move and opened her eyes, staring feverishly.

"God must punish me, not her, not her. Please God ..."

"Nonsense!" said Elizabeth flatly.

The brisk note in her voice jerked Eloise into full consciousness. The eyes cleared and focussed upon her.

"If anyone has sinned," said Elizabeth in the same matter-of-fact tone, "it certainly isn't you, my friend, and the good God, he will know this as he knows everything."

Eloise reached a hand toward her and Elizabeth took it between her own.

"You believe this?" asked Eloise faintly.

"Of course I do," said Elizabeth firmly.

"Then you forgive me?"

"Forgive you? What have I got to forgive you?"

Eloise looked at her and smiled.

"You mean that," she whispered, "you really mean that. It makes me very happy. Pray for me, Elizabeth."

"If it will ease you, I will," Elizabeth smiled at her, "but to my mind there are others who need it more than you do, my dear. You have hurt no one."

"The baby," Eloise whispered very faintly, "Louisa ..."

"I stand for you," declared Elizabeth clearly, "I will see that she is not hurt whatever may happen and whatever I have to do. I promise you."

Eloise seemed to relax after this. Her hand felt limp in Elizabeth's, her eyes closed and she smiled.

"Edouard," she said after a few seconds, "you'll help."

"I'm here," he said, "I'll do all I can. Don't fret, my love."

His voice was calm but his expression was stony with grief. A change seemed to creep over Eloise's face like the shadow of a cloud over a field. Just at that moment, Madame Leroux peeped into the room.

"The priest, he has come," she announced. "I have put him in the dining saloon with his acolytes."

The doctor stood up.

"Take Madame back to the baby," he said, "and make sure that nobody sees her face."

"I will fetch her veil."

Madame tiptoed out.

"I hope you will stay till I come," said Massin at the door, "I have some instructions to give you about *la p'tite*. She is healthy enough but naturally she will be an easy victim for the disease. You must take the greatest care."

Elizabeth nodded, watching the still face on the pillow.

From her chair beside the crib Elizabeth listened to the movements in the next room. The chanting of the priest was clear enough and she could smell incense. It was less than ten minutes before Massin returned though it seemed longer. He was frowning and looked angry. He shut the door carefully and rushed into speech.

"I don't care for this at all," he said. "That priest he is trying to . . ."

He turned to Elizabeth, the vigour of his movements contrasting curiously with the quietness of his voice.

97

"The husband ... that creature! Would he have influence with the priests?"

He spat out the words contemptuously.

"He is deep in with the Orleanists," Elizabeth answered. "It's more than likely."

"Just so. I might have expected something of the sort. His Reverence has been prying. He has been questioning the widow. She told me just now."

"What has she told him?"

"Who knows? Not she at all events. She talks like a river running. Enough, I suspect."

"Why?"

"He has just sent one of his acolytes away on some errand or other. I think, with a message."

Elizabeth rose, put on her black shawl and pulled down the veil.

"I'll take Louisa at once and go. Can you send someone for a cab?"

He smiled sardonically.

"I have already sent the widow. There are shawls and blankets enough to keep *la p'tite* warm and safe. I'll take you down now, while he is still at his mumbo-jumbo. I told her to bring the cab to the Rue St. Vierge, behind us."

As he spoke he was wrapping the baby in a blanket.

"I'll take her till we are downstairs. She must not start to cry."

They slipped into the vestibule and stood for a moment listening to the sounds which came from the sickroom then Massin beckoned with his head and led the way downstairs. He took her through a maze of courtyards and narrow, dark passages until they emerged into a back street. There was no sign of a cab.

"I must leave you," said Massin, "I had better be there

when they are finished. I have scribbled out a few instructions."

He thrust yet another paper at her and then placed Louisa gently in her arms.

"Madame Leroux will go with you," he assured her, "and when she comes back I will put the fear of the devil in her. She won't babble again, even to the priest, I promise you."

Elizabeth looked down at the tiny, sleeping face.

"I'll take the greatest care," she said.

"Of that I am convinced," Massin assured her drily, "or you would not now be holding her."

"One thing before you go. Will Eloise . . . can she say . . . I mean will she trust him . . ."

He frowned.

"I do not think he will make use of any confession, he cannot, you know: but in any event she is sinking fast. When I left she could not speak at all and she was barely conscious. Ah, here is the cab."

He waved and the driver drew up. Madame Leroux, inside, took Louisa and Massin helped Elizabeth climb in beside them. Before he could close the door she leaned out.

"Tell the driver, Notre Dame. I'll take another cab from there."

He nodded approval of this precaution and gave the driver his instructions.

"And, Dr. Massin, please would you let me have your direction."

"Why?" he demanded brusquely.

"I might need to consult you. I have no doctor in Paris and now there is the baby."

He raised an eyebrow.

"Mine is scarcely a fashionable practice."

"Nevertheless," said Elizabeth, "I prefer to choose a medical man for reasons which have little to do with fashion."

He shrugged and smiled.

"If you insist, Madame will tell you. I have no card. But remember that a connection between us might be dangerous. Goodbye."

He shook Elizabeth's hand, closed the door and in a few seconds the elderly cab-horse was clip-clopping into the boulevard.

Elizabeth saw the impressive front of the cathedral with relief. It had been an uncomfortable journey. Madame had wept incessantly for her mistress and for the baby. Elizabeth enquired delicately if she were provided for and found this a useful distraction for Eloise had been generous. Madame planned to buy a café in Rouen, her birthplace, which she would run with the help of her daughter-in-law, now widowed like herself.

"And the good doctor, he says I must go there today, I may not even see my poor mistress put into the ground."

Elizabeth comforted her in a fresh outburst of weeping and reflected privately that this was a wise precaution to take. She promised to visit Rouen some day to give Madame news of Louisa and to patronise the café which was to stand in the most respectable part of the town and serve none but the most respectable of the citizens.

Once at Notre Dame Elizabeth took the baby and got out, instructing the driver to return to the Rue St. Vierge with the widow. Madame Leroux bade them both a tearful farewell and the cab rumbled slowly away with her. Elizabeth, uncomfortably conscious of a chill breeze which had sprung up, stood in front of the vast entrance and looked about her for a cab. There was none in sight so

100

she decided to look for someone who might be persuaded to find her one. There were two urchins playing in the gutter on the other side of the square while they waited for visitors to the cathedral who might throw them a few sous. She had just made up her mind to go over and make her request, and had, indeed pushed the veil off her face in order to do so, when a smart new cab came briskly into the square and drew up opposite the cathedral entrance. Hoping to obtain its services once its passengers had alighted, Elizabeth pulled the blanket up to protect the baby's face and moved out of the shelter of the porch to the edge of the pavement. The cab door swung open and a small, fattish man emerged ungracefully backwards. He turned round to speak to the cab-driver and Elizabeth found herself face to face with James Frobisher.

8

The clock in the square struck four and Elizabeth moved restlessly in her bed. Through the gap in the curtains she could see that the sky was already paling into dawn. Impatiently she pushed back the bedclothes and groped for the tinder-box to light her candle. She flung on a dressing gown and tiptoed out of the room making for the staircase which led to the floor above.

Upstairs, all was well. Louisa lay soundly asleep in the new crib beside the narrow bed on which lay the generous form of Marie-Joseph. Jacques had presented this placid young person to Elizabeth the evening before with pardonable eclat. A more suitable wet-nurse could not exist in Paris, he had assured her, and from the beginning it had been comfortingly evident that Louisa thoroughly agreed with him.

Elizabeth crept downstairs again but she did not go back to her room. Instead she took the candle into her little parlour and lit the gas-light above her desk. Pulling a sheet of paper towards her she dipped her pen and began:

Dawn. Tuesday.

My dear Hector,

So much has been happening today, or rather yesterday, that I cannot sleep, so I have risen with the first light to

102

tell you all about it. By the time you receive this you will know that Eloise is dead ...

She wrote busily for some minutes describing the events in the Rue des Saintes and then paused, staring into nothingness with a faint smile on her face.

... if anyone had told me while I was standing outside the Cathedral that within a few minutes I would be hard put to it to keep my face straight I would not have believed them, but it was the case. James was so taken aback when he saw me, not to mention the baby, that he could do nothing but splutter and gobble at me. This was fortunate as I had a second or two to think up some cock-and-bull story about a cousin in America who had died in Paris on her way home after the death of her husband and how I was sending the child home to Skye. As a story it left a good deal to be desired, but I jumped into the cab before he had time to question me too closely and left him standing. I told the driver to drive to the railway station, and then altered my instructions later. What worries me most is that James and his wife have been invited to the Embassy tonight and are sure to meet de M. I don't trust James to keep quiet about what he saw. . .

The letter was never to be finished. The clock in the Square had struck five and the daylight coming between the curtains was beginning to make the gas-light look yellow and pale. The sound of a fast-trotting horse could be heard coming closer and closer. Elizabeth raised her head from her letter in surprise when the hoof-beats slowed to a halt outside the room where she sat. She pulled the curtain aside to look out and saw a cab standing at the kerb. The driver was in the act of climbing down from his perch. With a sudden surge of delight and surprise Elizabeth recognised the well-worn trunk roped on to the roof. Hector was back. She bundled the sheets of her letter into a drawer and then ran downstairs, her dressing-gown flying behind her, and made for the front door. Here she found Jacques, unbolting and unchaining the outer doors as if a dawn arrival was a matter of course to him. His dress was immaculate, his shoes polished. Only the grey stubble on his chin betrayed him.

"Good morning, Madame," he remarked, "one perceives that M'sieu Lacombe is arrived."

He flung open the double doors with a flourish but there was no one waiting on the step. The cab driver had the trunk upon the pavement together with various bags and valises and was leaning into the interior of the cab loudly informing the unseen occupant that, "One is arrived, M'sieu!" He looked around at the noise of the opening doors and came swiftly up the steps.

"M'sieu is not well," he announced without ceremony, "He is not drunk as I first thought for there is no smell of wine and he burns with fever and talks wildly of being a murderer."

Jacques gently restrained Elizabeth from running down the steps.

"Madame is not clad for this cold," he reminded her, "if she will rouse Catriona I will assist this good man to bring Monsieur inside."

Elizabeth obeyed at once and when she came back with a drowsy and bewildered Catriona, Hector was slumped on the carved settle in the hall with Jacques anxiously regarding him while the cab driver struggled up and down bringing in the luggage. Catriona took in the situation and sleep dropped from her. She felt Hector's forehead and then opened his shirt to examine his chest. Finally she bent over and sniffed at his breath. She shook her head anxiously.

"We must be getting him into his bed," she declared. "He's in a high fever."

"I will prepare a room at once," said Jacques who had paid off the driver and was gently edging him out of the door.

"No," said Elizabeth. "Mine is already aired and warm. Put him in there. Better than keeping him here until another is got ready."

She took Hector's hand and almost started at the dry heat of it. He opened his eyes and focussed them with difficulty on her anxious face.

"Sorry, my dear," he muttered hoarsely, "not the home-coming I had hoped for."

Elizabeth touched his cheek.

"It's good to have you back, anyway."

It did not take long for the three of them to get Hector into Elizabeth's bed. He submitted with a weary docility to their ministrations and when he lay semi-conscious among the pillows Catriona, the basin of washing-water perched upon her hip, looked at him narrowly and declared,

"We must be having the doctor."

Jacques who was attempting to persuade the patient to swallow some spoonsful of broth looked up at this.

"I know of a most excellent man, not ten minutes from the door. He attended my late master till he died and he was physician to the late Duc de Sailles and his poor wife."

"No need to be giving the master up for dead!" remarked Catriona tartly. "Are you not knowing one whose patients are still alive?"

"I would like you to send to this man," Elizabeth intervened hastily and gave Jacques the note to Dr. Massin which she had just written. He raised his eyebrows almost into his hair when he read the name of the district, but handed the broth to Catriona and left the room without a word.

It was almost eight when Massin arrived and Hector was perceptibly worse. Elizabeth rose to greet the doctor as he entered the room.

"I did not expect to have to call on you so soon."

He looked at the man in the bed.

"You had reason enough," he replied and began at once to examine him.

Afterwards he left Catriona by the bedside and beckoned Elizabeth to come outside. She took him into her little parlour where he went at once to the window and looked out at the garden.

"Your husband has the jail-fever," he said bluntly, "It's prevalent in Russia."

He turned and looked at her.

"You must realise already that he is very ill."

Elizabeth nodded.

"He will need the most careful nursing. I will write a list of what you and your woman must do and I will send over a cooling draught which will ease him. When I have seen the rest of my patients I will come again. Have you pen and paper?"

She indicated her desk and Massin sat down to write.

"Send out for these things if you do not have them in the house."

He handed her a short list and Elizabeth at once sent for Jacques who took the paper and in a few minutes she saw Régine run down the road. The doctor finished his instructions at last and looked at her closely.

"You must not distress yourself so, Madame. He is young and strong and this is important for the disease. He has no weakness of heart or lungs which might complicate things. In a day or so the rash will appear and he will be easier, I promise you."

Elizabeth nodded.

"And it will be a comfort that you may help him by doing exactly what I have written down. You are not helpless, as one is too often in the face of illness."

His face looked for a moment as it had done the day before when he had been sitting beside the dying Eloise.

"There is the baby," Elizabeth jerked out. "She cannot stay here."

Massin frowned.

"Even if you had not sent for me I must have written to you today," he said, "I was going to ask you whether you could not get the baby to England without delay."

Elizabeth's heart turned over.

"Why? What has happened?"

"It was just as I thought. The priest did send for the father. She died before he came. I left when I had done all that I could for I knew he would make the arrangements. He did not speak then, but he came to my rooms last night, very angry and demanding to know what had become of the child. The widow did not leave for Rouen soon enough."

"What had she told him?"

"Nothing more than that there was a child. He had found the crib."

"I see. And what did you say?"

"Just that I had delivered her of a child and that my patient had arranged for friends to take care of it, as she did not care to entrust it to her family."

"Why anger him unnecessarily?"

Massin shrugged.

"Why not?" he asked, "The damage was done. He

blustered and threatened but I played the dolt and he left. But not long afterwards this arrived."

He handed her a note.

"It was brought by a liveried servant who sat down in my room without permission and informed me that he had been instructed not to leave without an answer." he said drily, "He had a certain resemblance to a gorilla so I wrote one."

The note was short and very much to the point.

M. de Mavanne presents his compliments to Doctor Massin and would be glad to have news of the whereabouts of his daughter. He trusts that Doctor Massin for his own sake as well as that of the child will co-operate in this matter.

"His daughter," breathed Elizabeth.

"Precisely. His daughter."

"What did you answer?"

Massin moved his shoulders uncomfortably.

"I would have liked to have told him exactly what I thought of him but I realised this would be foolish. I was polite and very professional. Regretted I could not be of more help in the matter but all I knew was that the child had been taken away just before Madame de Mavanne's death by a tall veiled woman who spoke with a strong Gascon accent."

"Thank you," said Elizabeth drily.

He grinned momentarily.

"I remembered her telling me once that she had a nurse who came from Gascony and I thought this might start a hare."

"I hope it does."

"And I hope that this visit of mine doesn't put the cat

among the pigeons. I still think it would be best and safest for you to send the child to England if you can."

Elizabeth put her hands to her cheeks.

"I will try to arrange something," she said.

After Massin had left Elizabeth went back to Hector. He was restless and semi-delirious and Catriona was already carrying out the doctor's instructions and wiping his hands and face with cold wet cloths which she wrung out in a basin cooled with ice. Jacques had lost no time in supplying all that was needed. Elizabeth promised to relieve her in a short-time and went back to her parlour where she sat down and tried to think what was best to be done. A dozen hare-brained schemes passed through her mind, such as smuggling the baby out in a washing basket, but none of them were really practicable. She was still trying to see a way out of the dilemma when Jacques came in.

"Madame," he began, dramatically, "one watches this house. Behold."

He sidled to the windows which overlooked the Square and indicated a figure, shabbily dressed who leaned against one of the plane trees and smoked a pipe.

"And in the lane behind the house there is a mender of chairs. I would not trust myself to his chairs, me. He spends too much time with his eyes on the windows of the house."

Jacques straightened the muslin curtain.

"Moreover, Régine informs me that she was accosted by that species of animal, there below."

He jerked a contemptuous chin at the stalwart in the Square.

"She tells me she refused to listen to him and this I believe, but ... but another time he may catch her when

I am *not* waiting with impatience at the door for what she has to bring and then ..."

He shrugged.

"All the world has a price, Madame."

Elizabeth stared out of the window trying to grapple with this extra complication and Jacques edged a little nearer.

"I ask myself why, Madame."

Elizabeth made no answer.

"I consider that it is not that Madame does not trust me but that the secret is not hers to share. Is this the case?"

Elizabeth nodded. Jacques made a sweeping gesture.

"In that case," he announced, "I may put Madame's mind at rest. She may share her confidence with me for I have guessed her secret, me."

Elizabeth stared at him, and he nodded importantly.

"I recall that species of animal out there was once and may still be a footman in the service of M'sieu de Mavanne. I recall certain 'on dits' which preceded the arrival of Madame in Paris. I recall with great interest the wealthy aunt who died and the cutting which was taken from the newspaper. Me, I add two and two and I find eight. Is *la petite* the child of the runaway Madame de Mavanne, perhaps?"

Elizabeth nodded, speechlessly.

"And M. the doctor Massin attended this poor lady in her extremity? Ah. It was perhaps a little foolish to send for him. But we may yet contrive. *La petite* must of a certainty be sent to England where she will be safe."

"How?" demanded Elizabeth. "I have been trying to think of a way all morning."

"I will give the problem my attention, Madame. Do not disturb yourself further."

On this superb note he bowed and departed. Elizabeth

hardly knew whether to laugh or give way to a sneaking sense of relief that the matter was no longer entirely her responsibility. She rose and went back to Hector. He had fallen into an uneasy sleep and was tossing in the wide bed. Catriona indicated the sponges and the basin in which ice clinked and whispered a promise to return as soon as she had eaten.

Elizabeth tidied the rumpled bedclothes. Suddenly Hector's eyes opened, staring unfocussed at the ceiling.

"Clothilde," he muttered, "I'll see Clothilde. Perhaps it's too late, she'll know. Clothilde ..."

Elizabeth, conscious of a stab of dismay which startled her, wrung out the sponge in the basin. She could not recall that Hector had ever mentioned a Clothilde.

"If you see Dodon," remarked the hoarse voice beneath her hand, "tell him ... but Clothilde knows I am coming. I wrote. She knows how important it is. I must see Clothilde ..."

After this outburst the doctor's draught seemed to take effect and he slept. Elizabeth spent an unpleasant hour sitting in the chair beside the bed telling herself fiercely that she had no right, none in the world, to be hurt, or to be angry. They were strangers. Such emotions were not in the bargain. In any event Clothilde could be ... it simply did not matter who Clothilde might be and it was no conceivable business of hers. She resolved to think no more of the matter and returned to sponging the dry hands and the burning forehead. She was recalling, rather desolately, certain passages in Hector's letters which might, which could ... when the door opened and Jacques came softly in.

"A Madame Frobbeesher to see you, Madame. I have taken her to your small salon."

111

"Did you tell her about M'sieu? About the infection?"

"I did. She snap her finger and say Pooh!"

"An old lady?"

"No, Madame. Not young, not old, but large, of an enormity, I assure you."

"Stay here till Catriona comes back," said Elizabeth. "I'll see her."

This must be James' wife, and she must discover if she could, just what James had given away of yesterday's encounter. A connection with Massin could be a coincidence. To have been seen with a baby was evidence. And de Mavanne had the law on his side.

James' wife was indeed "of an enormity". In pink silk with much blonde lace trimming over a seven-foot hoop she filled the small salon much as a doll fills a box. She turned from the window when Elizabeth entered and curtsied vastly. Then she smiled, revealing a row of singularly beautiful teeth.

"Mrs. Lacombe?" she asked. "I am your new cousin, Joanna."

Elizabeth looked at the square, plain face, the shrewd grey eyes and the abundant fair hair and the first thought which came into her mind was that James had been luckier than he deserved, and probably a lot luckier than he thought.

"I am so glad to meet you at last," said Cousin Joanna, "we have been in Paris for a sennight and I was beginning to think I never would. I fear James' rejection still rankles."

Elizabeth was startled. This was breaking the ice with a vengeance, but the twinkle in the grey eyes was unmistakable, and irresistible. Elizabeth blushed and laughed back at her.

"I wish you will sit down."

Joanna regarded the frail and elegant chairs about her with a certain suspicion and chose to settle her ample form upon the window seat. Elizabeth sat beside her.

"I meant that we should come as soon as we arrived in Paris but James could always find something else to do. Yesterday nothing would please him but he must see Notre Dame."

"You did not go with him?"

"Cathedrals bore me," she said simply, "but now I wish I had. Cousin Elizabeth, it is conformable for me to call you that. I imagine, I must be twice your age."

"Of course," said Elizabeth, "and you will be Cousin Joanna. I am sure we will be friends."

Joanna took her hand.

"Now that is good of you. Tell me, Cousin Elizabeth, is your husband very ill?"

"Yes," said Elizabeth baldly, "very ill indeed. He has the jail-fever. He caught it in St. Petersburgh, it would seem."

Once again Jacques appeared silently at the door. Elizabeth jumped up but Jacques made an elaborately calming gesture.

"Be tranquil, Madame. M'sieu sleeps and Catriona is with him. Madame has another caller."

He fixed a meaning gaze on Elizabeth's face.

"M'sieu de Mavanne is below. He called to pay his compliments on M'sieu's return and now wishes to present his condolences to Madame."

Elizabeth hesitated.

"I will show him up, Madame."

"But Jacques, I do not wish . . ."

With an apologetic glance at Joanna, Jacques began to speak in French and very fast.

"See him now while your friend is here, Madame. I have

113

not told him she is here and he can do little as long as she is with you. If you deny yourself now he will come back. If you see him he cannot come again while your husband is ill. It would be odd, unmannerly ... you understand?"

"Oh, very well."

Jacques left the room and Elizabeth turned to Joanna.

"We have another visitor," she explained. "Have you met M. de Mavanne? He has come to enquire after Hector."

Joanna frowned.

"Yes, I have met him. Last night at the Embassy. In fact I ..."

At this point de Mavanne was ushered in by Jacques. He was a tall, saturnine man in his fifties with a deeply lined face which had a permanently discontented expression. He checked at the sight of Joanna in the window seat but then came in and kissed hands politely.

"Madame Lacombe, my condolences on your misfortune. I trust your husband will soon be well again. Madame Frobbeesher, a pleasure to meet again so soon."

Joanna bowed stiffly. De Mavanne's English was correct but heavily accented. He turned to Elizabeth.

"I was desolated to hear of your husband's illness, Madame. I do trust that it is not serious?"

"Serious enough, M'sieu, and most infectious."

"So distressing. But you have your kind cousins to support you through such an ordeal. How fortunate."

Elizabeth agreed.

"And you have a good doctor?" he asked solicitously, "After so short a time in Paris perhaps you would like me to commend one to you?"

"You are very kind," Elizabeth's voice betrayed none of the apprehension she felt, "but we have secured a most competent person. He has my complete confidence."

"That is so important. Might one enquire the name of this paragon? I may know of him perhaps."

Elizabeth rose and pulled the bell.

"I have to admit, M'sieu, I cannot tell you. My admirable Jacques sent for him early this morning when we discovered that my husband was ill."

"Ah, a veritable treasure, that man."

"Very true, M'sieu."

Jacques appeared with a tray of refreshments and de Mavanne breaking into French demanded the name of the doctor in which they all appeared to have such great faith. Jacques, pouring out madeira, replied fulsomely with details of lifelong friends of his who had been saved from certain death by this undeservedly obscure practitioner and expressed his ambition to have this genius recognised, nay famous ...

"He may yet become ... well-known," interrupted de Mavanne, and there was the hint of a threat in the smooth voice. It did not go unnoticed by Joanna who was watching the scene closely.

"And the name of this paragon?"

"Massin, M'sieu ..."

"Indeed," de Mavanne smiled, "I believe I have already heard that name."

He drank a glass of Madeira, made a few random observations and prepared to take his leave. Elizabeth rose with a heartfelt relief, to ring for Jacques to show him out. While they waited he expressed his condolences once more.

"And of course it must be so much more difficult for you with an infant in the house."

Elizabeth felt an icy hand take a firm clutch on her

bowels and hoped that her face did not betray this. In a voice creditably full of bewilderment she asked,

"An infant in the house, M'sieu?"

De Mavanne shrugged but his eyes did not leave her face.

"My apologies, Madame, but I understood from M'sieu Frobbeesher . . ."

"Ah, you must mean my poor cousin's child!" exclaimed Elizabeth. "No, she is no longer here. I put her on the train to Le Havre yesterday in charge of a nurse. I am spared that at least."

She smiled engagingly at him.

De Mavanne bowed.

"I understand, Madame. I understand perfectly."

When Jacques had shown him downstairs Joanna stood up to take her leave.

"You will be wishing me at the devil I dare say, so that you can return to cousin Hector. I hope I may come again?"

"Indeed you may. I'll be delighted to see you as often as you care to come."

Together they moved out to the head of the staircase and began to go down. From the upper landing came the unmistakable wail of a hungry new-born infant. Joanna paused and raised her eyebrows at her horrified hostess.

"Le Havre must be much nearer than I thought!"

9

Joanna removed her pink silk bonnet again and swung it by the ribbons.

"Last night, that man," she jerked her chin towards the front door which had closed behind de Mavanne only just in time, "that man spent more than half an hour with James, talking of you."

Elizabeth stood very still.

"James gave away a good deal, one way and another," said Joanna, "when he began fathering the child on your father-in-law I thought it time to bring him away."

"He would think that, of course, after what his mother told him."

"It's no business of mine, I daresay," Joanna went on, "but I didn't like de Mavanne, or the questions he asked. It occurred to me, I don't know ... Cousin Elizabeth, are you in any kind of trouble?"

Elizabeth nodded her head slowly.

"Look, let me help if I can," Joanna begged. "In an odd fashion I owe you an enormous debt."

"You owe me a debt?"

Joanna laughed.

"You got me out of a trap. I ... can't we sit down again and I'll explain and you can tell me what's wrong, if you want."

Explanations were made over a luncheon. Joanna for

all her vast bulk ate very little and Elizabeth for a variety of excellent reasons had little appetite.

"You see," said Joanna, "I never expected to be married. I was always fat and plain as a plate. No one looked my way. When mother died I took her place and kept house and my sisters got married one after the other. I stayed with Father and pretended even to myself that I didn't mind. You know, it's funny when I think of it. It was all so sudden. Less than a year ago I had made up my mind that I would be fat Aunt Jo for the rest of my life. Then my father went to Brighton for a week for the seabathing. He came back with this woman, Mrs. Simmons, a widow. He informed me he was going to be married again. I don't know why, but I had never thought of this happening. Mrs. S. took one long look at me and decided that the house was not big enough to hold both of us."

Joanna laughed.

"We were by far too alike. She made up her mind that I would have to go."

"What!" exclaimed Elizabeth.

"Oh, she didn't put it quite like that. What she did was to say to my father that it would be a good idea if *their* wedding was postponed till mine had taken place."

"What did your father say?"

"Oh, he pointed out the fault in such a scheme. That no one actually wanted to marry me. But my new mama was not to be floored by anything so trivial, not she. She was a friend of Mrs. Frobisher and so she knew of James and also how he was so indignant with you. Of course he was ready to leap into matrimony with anyone who could support him and his mother. Now Papa is really very well-to-do and Mrs. S. didn't lack for money, my father is her third husband and they have all cut up handsomely. She made him come down with a really lavish settlement and gave me some more from her own portion. I got more than twice what my sisters did."

She put back her head and roared with laughter.

"They were cross as crabs, what with the money and not being able to get me to come whenever they needed a nurse or a housekeeper. Here I am, married and independent when I never hoped to be. That's my debt to you. If you hadn't slapped James' face for him, he would never have married me."

"I wouldn't say that I had played a really active part in promoting the match," observed Elizabeth wrily.

"Well, you can be grateful to a tree which shelters you," said Joanna, "even if it never knew you were standing underneath. Now what's your trouble? Would you like to tell me?"

Elizabeth explained briefly: she showed Joanna the letter Eloise had written to Hector and described what had passed in the Rue des Saintes the day before. Finally she led her to the window and showed her the man in the Square, waiting and watching under his chosen plane tree.

"Surely you could ask the Embassy to help?" suggested Joanna.

"We might, if it was anybody else. But it's de Mavanne, you see."

"I don't."

"He's a very important man in the Orleanist party here, he's a Royalist ... they want to bring back the King."

Joanna stared.

"What king?"

"The Bourbon."

"Oh, French politics bamboozle me," said Joanna impatiently, "I thought they had a republic or something."

"So they have."

"Well, why can't you ask the Embassy?"

"Because it doesn't look as if the Republic is going to last very much longer."

"So?"

"Lord Normanby, the Ambassador, would like to see a monarchy in power."

"What business is it of his?"

Elizabeth shrugged.

"It's complicated. The Queen would like to see a nice respectable monarchy here instead of this low Republic. One of the Queen's equerries is Lady Normanby's brother, and Lady Normanby ..."

"... is a grey mare in the stable. I begin to see."

"So you understand I can't ask the Normanbys or anyone at the Embassy for help because they won't risk offending the party they hope and believe is going to be in power very soon. If I did I think they would hand Louisa over to de Mavanne with profuse apologies and Hector would be sent home in disgrace or even handed over to the French authorities charged with abduction."

"Surely they wouldn't go as far as that?"

Elizabeth looked uncomfortable.

"Well they might. You see Hector and his father are hand-in-glove with Lord Palmerston at the Foreign Office and Pam wants to see Louis-Napoleon stay in the saddle."

"That's the Prince-President or whatever they call him, isn't it? The one who's Boney's nephew."

"That's right. Some people think he's planning to bring back the Empire. Pam does. So do the Normanbys and they know Pam would like this. And Pam knows that they are hand-in-glove with the Orleanists because Hector tells him so. Why do you think Lord Normanby had Hector sent to Russia? They'd take any reasonable excuse to be rid of him."

"My dear, good girl," remarked Joanna, "you are in a pickle and no mistaking the matter."

"And now Hector's laid by the wall just when everything's happening at once. De Mavanne's only got to get a whisper of proof and he'll have the gendarmes in and then my tale will be told. The Embassy won't help."

Joanna got up and stalked round the table, her vast skirts swaying from side to side.

"We can't allow that. We can't. There must be something we can do."

"I've been thinking and thinking," sighed Elizabeth, "trying to find a way out and I can't. I feel like a mouse in a barrel."

Jacques entered with a note on a tray. It was directed to Hector in a flamboyant hand, sealed with green wax on which an elaborate design of hearts and roses was impressed around the initial C. It smelt of violets.

"I am just about to go up to him. I'll give it to him if he can read it."

Elizabeth's voice was a masterpiece of unconcern. Joanna looked quizzically at it but made no comment. She picked up the pink bonnet from the chair where she had laid it and began to pull on her gloves.

"I am sure we'll find a solution. May I come back later?"

Elizabeth took the outstretched hand and kissed the plump cheek.

"I hope you will."

Jacques intercepted his mistress as she was about to go upstairs.

"Is it that you have confided in your Cousin?" he demanded in an undertone.

Elizabeth nodded.

121

"She heard Louisa crying. Please ask Marie-Joseph if she will keep the door shut."

Jacques' face assumed a curious expression which Elizabeth could only describe as gleeful satisfaction. He nodded and bowed and went back to the small dining salon to usher Joanna to the door.

Upstairs, Hector was feverish and restless. He was muttering gibberish and picking at the sheet. Catriona looked tired and worried.

"He is no better, at all," she admitted, "his fever is worse and it is out of his senses he is, most of the time."

"Go and rest. I'll stay with him till the doctor comes."

Catriona left and Elizabeth began the endless sponging by which she hoped to keep the fever within bounds. After about half an hour he opened his eyes and said he was thirsty. There was lemonade on the table ready to hand. After he had drunk he seemed almost lucid.

"There's a letter for you," she told him clearly.

He put out a hand and took it from her but she had to open it for him and even when it was unfolded he thrust it back at her with a weary, impatient gesture.

"Can't see it. You read." he muttered.

The writing was elaborate but careless as if the note had been written in a hurry.

Rue Bercy.

Cheri,

I heard you were back. There are dragons round the house and I can't come to you. You must come to me. Come soon, it is very important that I see you.
thy Clothilde.

Elizabeth read this over and then remarked, calmly,

"It is from someone called Clothilde. She wants to see you as soon as possible."

The name seemed to upset Hector who soon relapsed into delirium. Again and again he implored someone, anyone to tell Clothilde, to see Clothilde. Elizabeth tried to calm him but he became almost violent, pushing her aside and trying to get out of bed. She rang for Jacques and between them they got him back beneath the covers. He was calmed by Elizabeth's promising to tell Clothilde ... an empty promise as she knew neither what to tell nor whom to tell ... and after another dose of the draught which the doctor had sent he fell into an uneasy sleep.

"The poor unfortunate!" remarked Jacques. "He suffers much. But be of good heart, Madame, the doctor will soon be here. I have sent for him."

"But he promised to call this evening in any event," protested Elizabeth, "why send for him specially?"

"Alas, Madame, we have yet another domestic crisis upon our hands," explained Jacques his face unnaturally serious; "your cousin, no doubt shocked beyond measure by the danger to poor M'sieu, has commenced in labour."

Elizabeth dropped the dripping sponge on the floor.

"She has what!"

"Her time is come, Madame. Her child comes some weeks early."

"But she didn't say she ... she isn't ... she can't ..."

"No, Madame? With such superb embonpoint is it not difficult to tell? At all events ..."

He retreated to the door.

"Madame your cousin has been assisted to the guest-chamber and has asked me to send at once for an *accoucheur*. I have summoned Dr. Massin in a note ... a perfect masterpiece that note; I am all helpless agitation, one would believe that I was expecting the birth of seven-

123

headed triplets. I am pleased it should be so widely circulated."

"What do you mean?"

Jacques shook his head.

"That Régine, she will not admit that she cannot read and so she was forced to ask the mender of chairs to read the direction. While I, imbecile that I am, in my agitation omitted to seal the note."

Elizabeth had been considering.

"Jacques, you can't. It isn't ... I mean ... my cousin did not even meet her husband until last January ..."

Jacques cast up his eyes.

"Poor man! That he should be so deceived. It is a wicked world."

With that he left the room and for the next hour Elizabeth was left to wonder exactly what scheme was being hatched. She had just made up her mind to summon Jacques and learn more, when the doctor arrived. Elizabeth heard the commotion and peeped from the window. This time Massin had taken a cab and was accompanied by a white-coiffed nun and a large leather bag. Almost at the same time Régine returned in another cab from which were unloaded a vast quantity of parcels and bundles. The loafer in the Square was enlisted by Jacques to carry a very heavy carved oak cradle up the steps into the hall and was thus privileged to hear the agitated accents in which Jacques implored the doctor to step upstairs immediately, but immediately, as matters had reached a point of crisis.

He was interrupted by a wail of dismay from Marie-Joseph who, leaning over the banisters, demanded shrilly that the doctor must come at once and speedily if he would be there before this blessed infant who was in such a hurry to be born. Before the front door was shut behind the loafer a final touch of verisimilitude was added by a prolonged bellow from Joanna in the guest-chamber and the sight of Dr. Massin taking the stairs two at a time.

Elizabeth sponging Hector once again listened to the commotion, uncertain what to think, or even what to believe. As Jacques had said it was hard to tell. Her uncertainty was ended by Massin who came in grinning broadly followed by Catriona.

"I am considering that I might make a living at the *Comédie*," said Massin. "What a pantomime. What a man."

The smile on his face died when he considered his real patient.

"I will not hide it from you, Madame, he is not better. You have a difficult time ahead of you."

When he had finished and had given instructions, Catriona took over the sickroom and dismissed Elizabeth.

"Away you, and hansel the mother," said she, "she's in the wee green room over the way. I've lent her a nightgown of my own but I'm nothing but a suspicion to that lassie. She's sent a note over to that hotel-place where they've lodgings. We'll have Mr. James on us before too long."

Elizabeth made for the door but was halted by a cry from Catriona.

"Mercy if I didn't forget. There's a woman to see you in the parlour. She's a nun, poor benighted creature ..."

Catriona sniffed. She had a poor opinion of Catholics.

The nun was in the window seat watching the comings and goings in the Square. When Elizabeth came in she got to her feet and looked at her warily.

"Madame Lacombe?"

"Yes, Sister. What can I do for you?"

125

Unexpected the Sister laughed. She seemed to examine her hostess closely.

"Mon Dieu, but you are not at all what one would expect."

Elizabeth might have made a similar observation but she was speechless.

"We heard our 'Ector had married an English girl chosen by his father and with much money, we looked at one another and said, Ah, what would you ... she will have many large teeth, no chest and a voice like a crane."

The Sister laughed again.

"It is always so in these family marriages, you understand, the marriages of convenience. But you are pretty, *enfin*, and you have style which is much more, and your teeth ... but they are charming. He is to be felicitated our 'Ector."

The teeth thus discussed were plainly to be seen for Elizabeth addressed in this uncanonical fashion was staring open-mouthed. Her visitor looked puzzled and a little hurt.

"What is wrong, why do you stare? So. Of course, you look at this absurd costume ... but it was necessary to come you understand and that no one should know me, so I found the good doctor and he brought me."

She contemplated her reflection in the mirror which hung over the chimney-piece.

"But it is becoming, no?"

By this time Elizabeth had taken in the delicately painted face under the linen coif, the white hands with their manicured nails and above all the scent of violets.

"Are you ... you must be Clothilde."

The robed figure turned from the mirror and came towards her with her hands outstretched and smiling gaily.

"Ah, the good 'Ector, he has told you of me, *enfin*. That makes my task easy. Now I need not explain. Take this."

She groped under the heavy skirts revealing pretty under-clothes which could never have belonged to any Order and produced a package of papers.

"You will charge yourself with this? I would have sent it with Dodon but when 'Ector wrote that he was to return I kept it for him to see, but now it must go and at once."

"Go?" asked Elizabeth bewildered, "Go where?"

"But London, my child, where else?"

When the door had closed behind Massin and his improbable companion Elizabeth made her way to the guest-chamber conscious of a perfect maelstrom of emotions which, she told herself firmly and repeatedly, had nothing to do with Clothilde, nothing whatever.

10

Elizabeth's attempts to expostulate with Joanna were a complete failure.

"But whatever can James say to this?" she protested, "I mean, you have made him either a wicked seducer or a cuckold. He isn't very convincing in the first role and he certainly won't relish the second."

Joanna snapped her fingers in a superb gesture of dismissal.

"James," she announced airily, "knows which side his bread is buttered."

Elizabeth, knowing the extent of James' debts was forced to admit that this was probably true.

"What do you intend to do now?"

"With my wedding tour interrupted in this untoward fashion?" exclaimed Joanna. "Go home immediately, what else? We will leave in two days with the utmost fuss and circumstance. Jacques has it all in hand. I will of course have to be carried down to the carriage and no doubt the gentleman under the plane tree can be pressed into service again. Marie-Joseph and little Louisa will travel with me and so will my maid."

"And what will *she* have to say to this masquerade?"

"Oceans, I've no doubt, but she loves a jest. I've written to her and told her to come to me here. She is to have known all along, you see."

Elizabeth stared.

"You mean to let James think that this is a real confinement? Oh, no, surely not!"

Joanna smoothed the sheet carefully.

"Be sensible, cousin. Would you place the smallest dependence upon James to carry through a stratagem of this nature without giving us away at the first check?" she enquired.

Elizabeth shook her head.

"I will undeceive him in London. He won't have too long to suffer the pangs of injured pride."

"It seems a little ... unkind," Elizabeth observed.

"It would be still more unkind to hand Louisa over to that creature without making a push to prevent it. Besides," added Joanna drily, "it's hard to be really unkind to James. He is armoured in vanity."

But neither indignation, nor injured pride nor incredulity was the dominating emotion in James' breast when he eventually appeared on the scene. Elizabeth was with Massin in the sickroom when Jacques announced that M'sieu Frobbeesher was in his wife's chamber and would be glad to see his cousin and the doctor.

In this, Jacques had exaggerated a little: James was far from glad to see either of them. He had placed himself by the open window of Joanna's room and awaited their entrance with a vinegar-soaked handkerchief firmly pressed to his mouth and nose. In his left hand was a large cheroot emitting thick smoke which he waved about from time to time.

Joanna lay in state among the pillows, splendid in silks and laces, her plump face composed in an expression which conveyed fragility and suffering bravely borne. Beside her, smelling-bottle at the ready, stood her maid, her boot-face preternaturally solemn though the prim mouth twitched at the corners.

James peered at them as they came in like a Turkish bride over a yashmak. From an impulse of sheer mischief Elizabeth walked briskly towards him her hand outstretched. James' eyes bulged like a coursed hare's and he looked imploringly at Joanna. His wife raised a languid hand.

"Poor James is so distressed to hear of Cousin Hector's illness ..."

"Ça ce voit!" muttered Massin.

"... but he has the greatest fear of infection."

"Quite! Quite!" spluttered James indistinctly, "exactly tho, delicate from a child, motht thutheptible, motht. M'mother would tell you, 'pon m'word!"

He retired yet further into the window behind a screen of vinegar and cigar-smoke.

"He is also anxious for my safety ..."

"Indeed?" said Massin with a glance at the open window.

"... and of course for that of dear little Louisa.".

It was evident from what could be seen of James' face that such solicitude on his part was by no means a certain thing but Joanna swept on smoothly.

"We have decided to return home and to continue with our tour when I have regained my strength. How soon will it be possible for me to travel, Doctor Massin?"

Massin shook his head and looked very serious.

"It is usual to advise that a lying-in be continued for at least three weeks."

James' eyes bulged over his handkerchief.

"A month, even, is not unusual."

James broke into a light sweat.

"But Doctor," he pleaded, "in the thircumthtanthes, the danger of infection, would it not be thafer ..."

Massin continued solemnly.

"But in view of the presence in this house of a serious fever, and the fortitude with which Madame has borne herself which displays, if I may say so, great strength of mind, not to mention the fact that the infant is obviously thriving with her present nurse ..."

He paused impressively.

"... it might, it just might be possible to permit a move to be made earlier. Shall we say in a week?"

James still appeared to be agitated. Joanna took a restoring sniff at her smelling-bottle and entered the argument.

"I cannot possibly risk exposing my dear ones to this fever a moment longer than is necessary," she declared, "whatever the risk to myself, I must insist on leaving this house and indeed this country, as soon as it can be arranged. Only in England shall we be safe. Today, I insist!"

She had recourse once more to the smelling-bottle.

"But no, Madame, today were suicide!" exclaimed Massin, entering into the spirit of the scene with a verve which gave Elizabeth the melancholy suspicion that he was enjoying himself, "I honour your sentiments in such a situation but at least one more day of rest after your ordeal is essential."

"Tomorrow, then!" murmured Joanna, faintly among the pillows, "I will not delay another moment!"

Massin took her wrist and stared at the ceiling as if seeking permission from a higher authority. James regarded the tableau with quivering anxiety.

"Perhaps," Massin said grudgingly, "if you have every care, every luxury ..."

Jacques coughed importantly from his post by the door.

"I will myself attend to this, rely on me, M'sieu le docteur, M'sieu Frobbeesher. The best of carriages, the fleetest of horses and a courier that I myself choose who will relieve you of all cares and smooth your path. You will have food of the finest and a basket of wines to sustain you on the voyage from M'sieu's own cellars."

James brightened a trifle.

"How soon can they be made ready?" asked Joanna wearily, her eyes closed.

"For Madame," announced Jacques impressively, "I can be ready tomorrow morning, early. In this way much ground may be covered in the cool of the day."

Massin nodded agreement. Everyone then looked at James who, disconcerted by their concentrated gaze, dropped his handkerchief and backed so far into the window that he nearly fell out of it.

"You are agreeable to this, M'sieu?" enquired Jacques.

"Of courthe, of courthe," stammered James, grovelling ungracefully for the handkerchief.

"Then we are decided. Mademoiselle Sproggins ..."

The boot-faced maid curtsied.

"Mademoiselle Sproggins will return to the hotel to attend to Madame's baggage and at half past seven in the morning the carriages will be at the door to take her and M'sieu up."

The question of the departure settled James took his leave with all the grace and ceremony of a rabbit started from its burrow by a ferret and those he left behind could give way to their emotions for a brief moment before the bustle of packing began.

In the hours which had elapsed since Clothilde's visit Hector had not at any time been sufficiently lucid to hear about the packet she had left. It seemed possible that Hector might have intended to send it with the Diplomatic Bag which would be safe from the inquisitive eyes of the *Bureau des Postes*. On the other hand those were not the only set of inquisitive eyes to be found in France who would be interested in the contents of a mysterious package. On an impulse, Elizabeth unlocked the drawer and drew it out; she opened the string binding and spread the contents on her desk. There were a large number of lists; military promotions, political appointments and diplomatic postings. Each name had a number after it. One or two of them Elizabeth recognised and knew them for supporters of Louis-Napoleon. All were recently appointed, the dates were written beside the names. She noted the large number of appointments in Paris itself and raised her eyebrows. Beside the lists there were a number of invoices for various consignments. The goods mentioned appeared innocent enough at first sight; tubing of various grades and sizes, lead sheets, and meal with the size of the grains carefully specified. There were also two travellers' samples. One was a scrap of heavy coarse serge dyed a dull blue, the other was a bunch of buttons in different sizes both bronze and brass with a spread eagle embossed on each. Attached to the last was a label which stated, "300 gross of each". The evidence seemed reasonably conclusive.

In front of her she had what amounted to proof that the Bonapartists were planning a coup. Proof was a different thing from the rumours and suspicions which had been rife in Paris for months. To the Republicans the papers in front of her would be proof of treason; to the Orleanists they would pose a real threat to their own hopes. It would be foolish, if not worse, to entrust such explosive material to an Embassy whose allegiances were known to be Orleanist. But somehow they had to be got to London.

Elizabeth bundled the lists and samples back into their wrapping and ran upstairs to the linen cupboard where she looked out a small cushion-case, waxed and waiting for the feathers gathered from the household's consumption of poultry. Catriona made and remade cushions twice a year. Needle and thread were to hand in the drawer. Swiftly Elizabeth filled the case from the feather-box. When it was well-plumped she shook off the clinging down, inserted the flat packet of papers into the very centre and sewed it up neatly and rapidly. In a drawer were embroidered cushion-covers; she chose one of gay, crimson velvet, slipped it on and sewed it up. The result of her work was a firm but comfortable cushion, ideal for travelling.

Marie-Joseph accepted her new destiny with undisturbed placidity.

"It is all one to me, Madame. I shall enjoy to see the world."

"You will take the greatest care, Marie-Joseph."

A smile spread over the broad-cheeked face.

"Madame need have no fear. Already she is like my own to me."

She had accepted the news that Louisa was to pass for Joanna's child with a similar calm indifference.

"My sister she takes my babe for hers," she had said, "her own being dead and with the blessed angels. For me I am content that they are in good care. It is all one."

The departure was impressive. Joanna and the baby together with Marie-Joseph and Georgina Sproggins occupied the foremost carriage, a vast and antiquated affair;

the courier, a harassed character with a sheaf of papers and a shrill voice, shared a coach with a mound of baggage while James and his valet brought up the rear in a light chaise. Joanna eyed its vast wheels and elaborate springing and designated it a "bounder". She predicted callously that James would be too travel-sick to concern himself much with the paternity (or, for the matter of that, the maternity) of the infant. Joanna herself reclined Cleopatra-style in the carriage, her head supported on a red velvet cushion and surrounded by every conceivable comfort from a large hamper laden with brandy, wine and delicacies to a pewter chamber-pot tactfully concealed in a leather-covered box.

Elizabeth entered the carriage to say her farewells and Joanna patted her cheek affectionately,

"Don't fret, my dear, I'll take the greatest care of Louisa. Just you forget about her and concentrate your attentions on that husband of yours. He's going to need all your care."

Elizabeth stammered her thanks.

"Nonsense," declared Joanna and leaned forward to embrace her. "You know, James has his good points. For example he has the most agreeable relatives."

The fortnight which followed was a waking nightmare. Afterwards, Elizabeth could remember very few of the details, but for the rest of her life certain sounds and smells could recall instantly for her the darkened, stuffy room where Hector tossed and muttered in the vast over-decorated bed. The clink of ice would remind her of the endless cloths wrung out in iced water for which Fernand fetched the ice twice a day. Massin would chase her out of the room to eat or sleep, or to take the daily walk in the park on which he insisted. Jacques went with her and once he had taken her into a tiny, dim chapel to light a candle for Hector's safe recovery. It had been oddly comforting to leave it burning there. Once she came out of the room to find Jacques and Catriona quarrelling fiercely in whispers and discovered that they were disputing who should sit up all night on the landing in case she should need one of them.

The nightmare deepened soon after that. Hector ceased to toss restlessly and talk wildly but lay in a kind of wide-eyed stupor while his fever mounted to a terrifying degree. Massin frowned and shook his head over him one morning and when he returned that night he declared that the crisis was at hand and that he would stay until it was past.

At dawn Hector had sighed wearily and muttered something while Elizabeth for the thousandth time was wringing out the cooling cloths in the water bowl. She jumped with apprehension for it was the first time he had made a sound for many hours. When she came back to the bedside, her skirt soaked in the icy water she had spilt, Massin was standing very still with his hand on Hector's pulse and his head bowed so that she could not see his expression. For one cold second she thought that Hector was dead but Massin raised his head to look at her and he was smiling.

"It's over," he said. "The fever has gone. He's sleeping. Look."

Catriona went weeping and rejoicing to spread the news and came back with Jacques who wept with her and embraced everybody, including Catriona, with great and Gallic fervour. After that he took command of the sick-room and chased all three of them into Elizabeth's parlour where Fernand, sleepy-eyed but smiling, brought them a lavish breakfast. Catriona put Elizabeth to bed where she slept the clock round, and woke to realise that the nightmare was over and that summer had come while she had not been looking.

The following afternoon she sat beside a weak but lucid patient who protested at being fed like a baby and insisted that Jacques come and shave him. This was the real evidence that his recovery had begun and she did not need Massin's delighted report when he came in during the afternoon.

After he had left she returned to the sick-room and found Hector sleeping peacefully. She sat down in the armchair and almost at once fell asleep herself. Over an hour later she woke with a start to find Hector propped up on his pillows and looking pleased and surprised. On the other side of the bed stood the reason. Lord Lacombe had arrived in Paris. She stared at him for a second, wondering confusedly if he were part of a dream.

"Wake up, girl!" said the familiar voice. "Asleep at yer post, hey?"

She could not answer him. To her shame and confusion she began to cry. Lacombe moved swiftly round to her side of the bed and pushed her back into the armchair.

"Hey, what's this? Not like you, girl. Never known you weep, never."

He thrust a large handkerchief into her hand and patted her shoulder.

"So pleased to see you," she managed to jerk out.

"Are you, indeed? Then I hope I'm never *unwelcome!*"

"So sorry . . . can't help it."

"'Course not, 'course not. Perfectly natural."

He rang the bell energetically and Catriona appeared almost at once.

"Bring a glass of wine, Katterin, the girl's got the vapours. Don't wonder at it."

He administered the wine gently and gradually her sobs subsided.

"Come, now, come, ye're upsetting yer patient. Won't do, ye know. Won't do."

And it was Hector's worried face among the pillows which brought her to her senses. She mopped her face, sniffed and began to laugh, rather shakily.

"After all this, to cry *now*. It's ludicrous. I'm so sorry."

She got up and held her hand out to her father-in-law.

"My actions belie my words a bit, but believe me I am *very* glad to see you, my Lord."

This dignified speech was spoilt by a hiccough which made both her hearers laugh. She blushed and fled to the door.

"I must look a perfect fright," she said and went.

That evening after Hector was settled for the night they sat together in the study and she poured out the story of the past weeks. It was not new to him.

"Saw Joanna before I left. Gave me a cushion!"

He twinkled at her.

"Good sort of a creature that."

"And what's your news?"

"Nothing good, nothing good. That cushion you sent ... Lord but you should have seen Pam's stiff-rumped secretary all covered with feathers like a moultin' hen ... thought Pam would be carried off, 'pon m'soul I did."

He chuckled happily.

"A thunderin' good notion for all that. Did you read the stuff in the packet?"

"Some of it. I take it we are to have a second Empire."

He blew out a cloud of cigar-smoke.

"Not unlikely," he agreed. "One way or another I don't

think the Republic will last much longer. What worries us, who's goin' to take its place. We got a notion from one of those letters that there's a bunch of scoundrels using our Embassy as a headquarters."

She looked at him startled.

"I know it's full of Orleanists. That's no secret to anyone, even the Republicans."

"Normanby's a fool. Nose-led by her Ladyship and she's a catspaw for those two at Windsor. Normanby thinks his Orleanist friends are all respectable Royalists. He'll get his fingers burned, you mark my words. Outsiders shouldn't meddle with French politics: too many wheels within wheels."

Elizabeth raised her eyebrows at this remark.

"And what is Pam up to, then?"

"Come, come, m'dear, no need to take that tone. There's a difference between backin' yer fancy as Pam's doin' and tryin' to nobble the favourite."

"Nobble!·Do you mean ... murder?"

Lacombe sipped his brandy and looked hard at her.

"Might amount to that. We'd a hint ... more than that," he admitted. "Not H.E. himself, of course, hasn't the guts. But he's made some odd friends recently."

"So that's why you're here."

He nodded.

"That and other reasons, good ones. Pam told me to see how the land lay and warn him off. Discreetly, of course."

"Of course," said Elizabeth mischievously.

"Impertinent hussy. I can be discreet if I see the need. Been in this game a long time. People think you're a blusterin' old fool and drop things. Don't have to wear a false beard an' smoked glasses to see what's under your nose, y'know."

She nodded penitently.

"I was worried about Hector. Joanna gave me a poor account of him. Might have known you'd do the trick all right and tight. And then there was your Aunt Frobisher."

"Aunt Frobisher? Is she not in Hampshire?"

"She ain't then. Back at Lacombe House. Boomin' about the place."

"But why?"

"Joanna don't want her livin' with them, can't blame her for that. Yer aunt's to move into the Dower House once they've put a roof on it and got rid of the rats. They were to go on this tour till it was ready. Now they're back and Joanna sent m'sister packin' up to Town to stay with me till it's ready."

He sounded so comically indignant that Elizabeth put her head back and laughed aloud.

"Now we come at the truth, my Lord. You are fled from Aunt Frobisher."

"Don't deny it. Dreadful, managin' female, m'sister, but had to oblige Joanna. Not much to do after all."

Elizabeth agreed fervently.

"She was a goddess out of the machine," she admitted, "I couldn't *think* what I was to do."

He looked at her affectionately.

"You've had too damned much thinkin' to do, if you ask me. Leave it to Hector for a bit. You look worn to a thread."

"It was such an ingenious scheme."

"Scheme's misfired a bit, y'know," said his Lordship, maliciously. "Take it ye haven't heard?"

"Has there been gossip? She said she didn't care for that but I had my doubts. There was James to consider..."

"No, no, we've kept it very quiet. They went straight

140

into the country, saw no one, went nowhere. The only people they saw were me and the doctor."

"The doctor? Louisa isn't ill?"

"No. No, thrivin'."

"Then why ... oh, *no!*"

Lacombe nodded.

"Just so, m'dear. She'll be confined in early November. There's been little gossip so far but to have an infant twice in the first twelve months is bound to occasion some comment, don't y'think?"

11

In a surprisingly short time Hector was up and about.
Before his father went reluctantly back to Lacombe House
and Mrs. Frobisher he was again at work. Elizabeth soon
found herself working with him, not only in the study
where she translated newspapers and wrote letters but in
her role as hostess. As soon as Hector had been well
enough to receive visitors they had flocked to the house.
Jacques, despite his avowed preference for a quiet house
was evidently in his element. The unused rooms were
opened and aired and the big dining saloon brought back
into commission for they rarely dined alone. Elizabeth
found herself busier than she had ever been in her life.
Jacques and Catriona quarrelled incessantly in the common cause of trying to prevent their one-time patient from
over-working, a task almost beyond them because it was
clear that political events in Paris were moving slowly but
surely towards a crisis. Hector was soon deeply engaged in
the delicate task of gathering information, sifting fact from
rumour and sending his findings privately to Lord
Lacombe. To obtain the information Hector had to pick
up the threads of his earlier time in the capital.

These threads led to some surprising conclusions. One
evening Jacques entered the study where Elizabeth was

reading and Hector compiling a report. For once he seemed a little agitated.

"There is a ... person ... to see Monsieur."

Hector did not look up.

"Yes?"

"He requested me to inform you that his name is Dodon."

Hector did look up at this and a grin spread across his face.

"I thought it best to take him to the kitchen," said Jacques. "He is there, eating. One might think he had not eaten for some time."

"He probably hasn't. Let him finish what he has, give him a glass of wine and bring him to me here."

"Here, M'sieu?"

"Yes."

"But ... Madame is here. He is not at all the sort of person ..."

"Madame will probably retire."

"Oh, will she?" said Elizabeth indignantly.

"And Jacques, see that no temptation is put in his way. He is a pickpocket."

Jacques breathed deeply.

"I had inferred as much, M'sieu. Perhaps M'sieu will be kind enough to request the return of my watch. It is admittedly of small value but it was a mark of esteem from my late master."

He withdrew in good order. Elizabeth put a marker in her book and got up.

"I had better leave you. It's time I went to bed."

Hector grinned at her.

"And we are alight with curiosity, aren't we?"

She made a face at him.

"Of course I am. Yesterday we have a woman whose occupation I dare not even guess at ..."

143

"She is a perfectly respectable lodging-house keeper."

"Then I doubt whether the same could be said of her lodgers. The day before it was a stall-keeper from the fruit market. Tonight it is a pickpocket. Tomorrow, no doubt we will have a murderer."

"Oh, he has already called, by the front door."

She gasped and Hector roared with laughter.

"It's a shame to tease you. I'll come in and say goodnight and tell you all about Dodon," he promised. "If I may."

"Of course you may, in fact if you *don't* . . ."

"Will you come and say goodnight to me?"

To her annoyance, Elizabeth found herself blushing at this suggestion and she left the room without another word.

Catriona was waiting for her in the big bedroom, now restored to Elizabeth's use. As soon as Hector had been on his feet again he had taken over the guest chamber for his own. Elizabeth sat down at the dressing-table while Catriona undid the forty little buttons down the back of her bodice.

"It'll have to be hoops tomorrow night, Catriona, we're going to the Embassy."

"Which dress will you be wanting?"

"The green silk. It's cool."

Catriona sniffed.

"It's new dresses you are needing with all this ceilidhing."

"I know. I must try to see the dressmaker in the morning. If she'll come."

"She'll come," said Catriona firmly, "I will be seeing her myself. There's the new muslin still to be made up and the blue silk. Fine you will look in that."

Elizabeth sat down in her shift and began to take the

144

pins out of her coronet of plaits. She pulled a silver tray towards her to put them in and saw an envelope lying upon it. While Catriona undid the thick braids and applied the brush, she unfolded it. It was from Massin.

"Why didn't you tell me about this?" she asked sharply. "When did it come?"

"Not an hour ago."

"Why wasn't it brought to me?"

Catriona shrugged.

"I was not wanting to disturb you and himself, in the wee room."

"Why ever not?"

Catriona brought the night-gown from the bed and put it over her arm while she untied the neck of the shift. The ribbon was knotted and Catriona muttered under her breath as she struggled with it.

"Well, Catriona?"

"Och, it's brother and sister you might be," she burst out, "him across the way and you lying awake half the night reading and wasting the eyes of you. That's not how things should be between you at all."

"Catriona! Will you be keeping your long tongue to yourself!" Elizabeth blazed at her. "It's no business of yours how things are between my husband and me."

Catriona regarded the flushed face in the mirror with a sapient eye.

"Och, och," said she, "so that's the way of it?"

Elizabeth rose and turned on her.

"What's the way of what?"

Catriona presented her with the night-gown and, as had been her custom since Elizabeth had ceased to be a child, turned her back while she slipped it on.

"It's a meddlesome, long-tongued cailleach I am," she

145

said drily, "but I am knowing a few things about you, mo chridhe."

"Oh, away with you to your bed!" rejoined Elizabeth angrily.

Once Catriona had gone, Elizabeth regarded herself in the mirror for a few seconds, made a hideous face at her reflection and then laughed. Feeling better for this odd exercise she jumped into bed and picked up her book. Before long she was interrupted by a tap at the door.

"Come in, if you're not Catriona."

"And what has that redoubtable female done now?" asked Hector, closing the door.

"She ... oh, never mind. Come and sit down and tell me what happened."

Hector obeyed.

"I am bound to say," he remarked, "that all this *bijouterie* becomes you much better than it became me."

He indicated the elaborate, gilded carving of the six-foot high, canopied bed-head: cherubs rioted among swags of fruit and flowers restrained only by love-knots, garlands and some exiguous draperies.

"It was no choice of mine," Elizabeth retorted. "It was in the house when you bought it. In fact I think the place was built round it."

"Knowing the reputation of the delightful creature whose house it was, I wouldn't be surprised if you were right."

Elizabeth looked primly down her nose.

"You should not say such things to a gently nurtured female."

"If one thing more than another reconciled me to marrying a gently nurtured female," returned Hector, "it was the conviction I could say just that kind of thing to her."

He smiled down at her and she felt suddenly shy and rather breathless.

"I had this note from Dr. Massin," she said hastily, "I think you ought to read it."

He took it from her and the smile faded from his face as he took in the few lines it contained.

I have had a visit from an official gentleman who enquired rather too closely for my comfort into the circumstances of the birth of a child to Mrs. Frobisher. I fobbed him off for the time being but the incident left me uneasy and I think you ought to know about it.

"I've been expecting something like this," observed Hector, "de Mavanne is back in Paris. I'm not sure where he has been but one of my visitors seems to think it might have been Gascony."

Elizabeth laughed.

"It worked! Didn't I tell you that Massin had tried to send him off on a wild-goose chase?"

"Did he indeed. He is a man of resource, our Edouard. But you must not worry about this. Louisa's safe enough."

"Of course she is. And what about the light-fingered gentleman? Have we any silver left?"

Hector laughed.

"Oh, he disgorged before he left. It's a game with him among his friends to see how much he can pouch during a visit. And what he brought me would have been worth all the silver in the house."

"Indeed?"

"It was a letter. He found it in the wallet of a man I was interested in."

"What did it say?"

"Nothing I hadn't already suspected but it is always helpful to have confirmation."

"Don't be tantalising. You wouldn't have come if you didn't mean to tell me."

He smiled.

"Wouldn't I?"

Elizabeth looked down at the embroidered hem of the sheet and could think of no answer to this.

"Are you going to tell me?" she coaxed.

"When I know a little more, yes."

"But how will you find out?"

"Ask me in the morning. I may need a little help from you. Don't worry, nothing more than an untruth or two."

She looked at him enquiringly but he just laughed at her bent forward and kissed her lightly on the cheek. She put up her hand to his face and he caught it and kissed the palm.

"Goodnight, my dear."

"Goodnight."

The door clicked to behind him. Elizabeth lay awake for some time remembering one Clothilde and wondering whether Hector had called at the Rue Bercy.

In the morning Hector did not appear for breakfast and Jacques informed Elizabeth solemnly that M'sieu was keeping his room that morning and was not himself, not himself at all. Alarmed at this news she left half-read the long amusing letter decorated with thumbnail drawings of Louisa which had come from Joanna and went to knock on the door of the guestroom.

"Hector, what's the matter? Aren't you well? Have you got a ..."

The words died on her lips. Hector was not addicted to the extremes of fashion affected by his cousin but he was usually neat and fastidious about his clothes. The figure which now confronted her was dirty and unkempt. He wore ill-fitting trousers stuffed into half-boots, and a dirty ragged shirt which displayed its patches and stains under a greasy striped waistcoat. His hair straggled uncombed from under a filthy peaked cap and on his chin was a day's growth of dark stubble. He grinned wickedly at her bewildered expression.

"I am to be Dodon's guest for today. His half-wit cousin. From Alsace. Which will account for my peculiar French."

He assumed an expression of bovine stupidity which made her giggle.

"Jacques did say that you were not yourself this morning."

"That man should have been in the service. Look, Liz, what I have to do today may take some time. Will you give it out that I have had a slight relapse. Nothing very serious but you thought I should keep my room. They all know I have a grey mare in my stable."

"If that were only true. What about the Embassy reception for the Turkish delegation tonight?"

"Would you mind going by yourself? Madame de Villette will chaperone you."

"No, I don't mind. I'll make my worries an excuse to leave early. But you will be back for La Clemenza tomorrow night, I hope. I'm looking forward to that."

"I'll be home tonight after dark. You come and say goodnight to me, this time. I like to see you *en grande tenue*."

The reception was crowded. The great rooms positively glittered with orders. Elizabeth arrived early to bear her part in the evening's work. After helping with the reception of the guests she slipped off to rejoin Mme. de Villette who had found her way to the cardroom. At once she started a minute inquisition into the course and cure of

149

Hector's illness. She then recommended a number of doctors in terms which made Elizabeth resolve privately to have nothing to do with any of them. She then demanded to know the name of the man they had employed.

"Me, I collect doctors, always in the hope that some day before it is too late I may find a good one."

It seemed a good opportunity to do Massin a good turn, though the idea of that saturnine young man cossetting a fashionable valetudinarian seemed a little unlikely. Elizabeth told Madame his name and direction while the prospective patient scrabbled in her reticule for a pencil. At the name of the district she looked up from the search.

"Where? He cannot but be a horse-doctor! The poor Hector. Why did you not consult me before you called in such a person. Who recommended him to you?"

Elizabeth thought quickly.

"It was an emergency. He was so ill. It was Jacques who knew of him."

"Ah. Ah, the good Jacques. He would have reason, that one. And he is competent you say?"

She found the little ivory tablets at last.

"We shall see what he can do for my neuralgia," she declared. "What name did you say?"

"Massin. Edouard Massin."

"An all too familiar name," said a voice behind Elizabeth. She turned to encounter the lined face of Pierre de Mavanne. Madame greeted him without enthusiasm.

"You have met M. de Mavanne of course?" she asked Elizabeth.

"I have indeed. Good evening, M'sieu."

He bowed over her hand.

"A pleasure to meet you again, Madame. And you

continue to employ Massin as a medical man, do you, Madame?"

. Elizabeth nodded.

"It is something of a coincidence. My late, unfortunate wife was also attended by this ... obscure ... practitioner. He must have great skill."

"I believe he has, M'sieu," said Elizabeth in a slightly bored voice.

"He also appears to have an ... individual, shall we say ... view of his responsibilities."

"Indeed, M'sieu."

Madame de Villette was looking from one to the other with the expression of a sparrow expecting crumbs.

"Did you not find this to be so?"

"He certainly impressed me with his skill and his devotion," said Elizabeth. "I am convinced that Hector owes his life to him."

"He certainly seems to owe him a great deal," agreed de Mavanne.

Madame de Villette, puzzled by the undertones of this exchange, attempted to change the subject.

"And how did you enjoy your visit to England, M'sieu? I believe you have not long returned."

He did not take his eyes off Elizabeth who received this news with a sinking in her stomach which she hoped was not reflected in her face.

"I found it a very interesting country," he admitted, "more interesting than I had expected. London was thin of company at this time of the year so I decided to visit the country. I stayed for a time in Hampshire. Do you know Hampshire, Madame?"

"No. Not at all," Elizabeth confessed, her heart beating very fast, "I believe it to be very beautiful."

"As so much of your country, Madame. But you will no

doubt see Hampshire for yourself when you visit your cousin. I understand he is now established there ... with his family."

"No doubt I shall," said Elizabeth stiffly.

"He has married a remarkable woman, your cousin," de Mavanne observed, "I venture to say, unique."

There was a tiny, ominous pause after this remark. It was broken by a slight commotion at the door of the cardroom. In the entrance, restrained by an outraged footman was a tall man in highly inappropriate checked trousers and a shabby grey ulster. Elizabeth knew him slightly for a hanger-on of the Orleanist clique. He was known as Polichon because of his enormous bony nose. He looked pale and dishevelled. He thrust the footman aside and looked round the room. His eyes met de Mavanne's and he gave a jerk of his head towards the hall. De Mavanne frowned and made an almost imperceptible nod. Elizabeth leaned over Madame de Villette's shoulder and pretended to take an interest in the cards she held but out of the corner of her eye she saw Polichon slip back into the hall. De Mavanne murmured an excuse and moved away. After a few moments Elizabeth saw him leave the room as well. Elizabeth took her leave of Madame as quickly as she could, choosing a moment when her friend wanted very much to continue with the game. Then she too slipped into the hall.

The hall was deserted except for two huge, bewigged, silk-stockinged footmen. A patter of polite applause came from the drawing-room. The Normanbys had engaged some singers from the Opera to entertain their guests. One of the footmen approached.

"Madame desires?"

"A cab, Giraud, if you please. M'sieu is ill and I must go home."

"I am desolated, Madame. I trust M'sieu will soon recover."

He nodded majestically at the other footman.

"A cab," he ordered loftily, "I will myself fetch Régine. If Madame will be seated."

He bowed her to a heavy carved wooden settle which stood between the door of the Ambassador's study and that of the anteroom. The door of the latter was slightly ajar. The chatter and laughter from the drawing-room died down as a few chords on the pianoforte introduced the next singer. In the comparative silence Elizabeth could hear voices in the anteroom.

"You are an imbecile."

De Mavanne's harsh voice was unmistakable.

"But I had to tell you, it alters all our plans!"

"You should never have come here ... and in those clothes. It was simply inviting attention."

"Do you think I should have written you a note? And let some flunkey carry tales to the old fool."

"You should have used your alleged brains. Shut that door!"

"But we will have to do something tonight ..."

Polichon's voice came nearer.

". . . and there is no time to spare."

"I've a mind to make one stone hit twice," said de Mavanne thoughtfully just as the door was closed. At that moment Régine arrived, her arms filled with wraps and the young footman returned breathlessly to say that the cab was waiting.

Once at home she went swiftly to Hector's room. He was there, his hair wet and wild from the bath and he was busy shaving.

"You look a trifle agitated," he said, wiping the foam from his face. "What happened?"

She sat down in the window and described her encounter with de Mavanne.

"He *must* realise now. And he's a dangerous man."

Hector patted his face dry.

"He can't do much, not to me. Think what Pam would have to say."

"I don't care what he'd have to say if you were ... were ..."

Hector began to subdue his hair ruthlessly with two brushes.

"So they don't want flunkeys to carry tales to the old fool," he remarked thoughtfully. "I would say that exonerated Normanby."

"But it does look as if they're up to something."

"Oh, they are, we knew that. It also looks as if they had heard already, which means they've got someone in the *gendarmerie*."

"Heard what?"

He grinned at her reflection in the mirror.

"Dodon and I have, er, nobbled an assassin."

She stared.

"We really meant to try and get him drunk and talkative," he explained, "but he wasn't the sort to get talkative when he was drunk. He just got morose and touchy. So, he started fighting. Dodon's girl fetched the police and now he's in jail with that *very* interesting letter safely back in his pocket. Dodon is a real artist. From what you tell me it looks as if the news has got back to his employers."

"Do you mean to tell me that de Mavanne is really involved in an assassination?"

"Up to his neck. I could prove it if I had to. He seems to have had this wretched creature brought from Italy to do the actual killing, and I imagine he bought the bombs

154

in London. We make a useful line in explosives at home, so the Italian told me."

"Bombs! Oh, how horrible!"

Hector nodded.

"I think that Louis-Napoleon was to be blown up on his way to the theatre tomorrow night. That would knock a Bonapartist coup into a cocked hat!"

"Blown up together with half a dozen perfectly innocent people who just happened to be too near. I do think that is a dastardly way to set about things."

Hector moved across the room to shrug himself into his dressing gown.

"How would you prefer to be murdered?" he asked sardonically, "A knife, or poison? I'll make a note of it."

She ignored the teasing note and moved restlessly to the dressing-table.

"Oh, you know what I mean. What will they do now?"

A familiar scent struck her nostrils and she saw the note lying open on the mahogany top, its flamboyant handwriting flaunting at her. A sentence jumped out at her before she could turn her head away. "... I wish, *mon amour*, that you could find the time to come again before I leave: I have a good deal to tell you ..."

"If the little assassin talks to the police," Hector was saying, "our friends may have to get out of France fast and that will solve our problem very nicely. On the other hand, the Italian may not know who is employing him. He seems to be very much the anarchist, talked of tyranny and the people, you know the style of thing."

"Yes, of course," Elizabeth spoke almost automatically.

"But if this is all part of a coup, and I think it must be, they'll have to think again ... find another way. They may even have to do their own dirty work. In that case I have people watching them and we'll soon hear of any developments."

He was talking more to himself than to her but at that point he caught sight of her white face.

"For Heaven's sake, what's the matter, Liz? You look positively hag-ridden?"

"Do I? I'm tired I expect. It was a bit ... difficult tonight."

He pulled her to her feet and propelled her to the door.

"Go and have a good night's sleep. Things will look less dismal in the morning, I promise you."

At the doorway she turned.

"Hector?"

"What is it?"

"What ... who ... that fight you spoke of?" she stammered losing her resolution at the last moment, "you didn't get hurt?"

He laughed at her.

"Don't worry. My part was less than heroic. When we saw how things were going we changed our tactics. We started to make insulting remarks about Calabria, that was where he was born, Calabrians and finally Calabrian women. He lost his temper and tried to strangle Dodon. I pulled him off so he went for me with a chair. All I had to do then was to lumber around between the tables in the café making nasty remarks which would keep him at boiling point until the police arrived and saw what he had done to the furniture of the café. It was perfect farce."

"But suppose he had hit you?"

"He didn't. Will you go to bed."

"Will you be called as a witness?"

"Not once they've found that letter," he said drily. "They'll have other fish to fry. Goodnight, Liz."

He pushed her gently out of the door. She had her hand

on the handle of her own door when he called softly after her.

"Liz!"

"Yes?"

"Thank you."

"What for?"

"Oh, just thank you. Lying's an ignoble occupation."

Warmed by this exchange she had almost shut the door when she remembered something.

"Hector, what do you think he meant by 'I've a mind to make one stone hit twice'?"

But the other door was closed.

12

The next day was unbearably hot for the Paris summer
was beginning to close down upon the dusty city. The gala
performance due to be held that night was unusual. Com-
monly, Paris at such a time was empty of the people who
made up its Society. This summer, however, the political
uncertainty had kept many of those concerned from their
cool, country houses. A delegation from the Sublime Porte
to discuss the deteriorating situation over the Holy Places
had embarrassed the French government, unwilling to
discuss future developments until they could be certain of
a future for themselves. The Turkish delegation found
themselves caught up in a round of hospitality and official
fêting which left them little time to discuss anything. A
gala performance of *La Clemenza di Tito* made part of
this round.

By mid-afternoon the sky above the city had turned
into a brassy dome and there was not a breath of wind
stirring. To the south the clouds piled higher and higher.
In the baking streets hardly a soul moved. Only the flies
were active, tormenting the wretched cab-horses, left to
stamp and swelter while their drivers found refuge in shady
cafés until the cool of the evening should liven up their
trade. The beggars slept in the doorways and even the
pigeons seemed torpid and sleepy.

At six o'clock Elizabeth came up to her room and regarded the paraphernalia laid out for her without enthusiasm. Heavy flounces of sea-green silk covered the bed and over the chairs were draped the heavily trimmed petticoats which would help to fill out the enormous skirt to its fashionable dimensions. Hanging from a hook on the door was the seven-foot wide cambric and whalebone cage on which all these would be laid. Elsewhere, wherever there was space, were shoes, gloves, scarf, stockings, underclothes. The copper water-cans stood ready to fill the bath and fleecy towels hung from the towel-horse. Amongst all this stood Catriona, her face hot and red from her exertions.

Elizabeth had her bath and Catriona patted her dry and handed her a silk shift. In the heat, even this garment, thin and transparent as it was, seemed oppressive. Elizabeth looked about her at the mass of materials she was expected to heap upon herself and rebelled. Catriona was already waiting to lace her into the heavily boned corset.

"No," said Elizabeth, "I won't. Not for twenty Turkish delegations and a hundred gala performances."

She pushed the corset aside and Catriona's mouth opened in dismay.

"Get out the white muslin I wore last summer. Cut off the black ribbons and put on the Indian scarf as a sash," said Elizabeth decisively. "And take that contraption away and burn it."

She pointed at the crinoline.

Catriona protested shrilly.

"You can't be going dressed like a schoolgirl and all the world in silks and jewels. What will Mr. Hector say?"

"He won't even notice, and if he does, I don't care what he says. Bring me the white muslin, if you please."

Grumbling and protesting, Catriona did as she was asked. Only on one point was she adamant. Elizabeth

159

must wear the stays. Only women of a certain kind would appear in public uncorseted and she would not be doing her duty if she permitted it. Elizabeth gave in.

When the muslin dress, hastily pressed, was on, the gay sash carefully tied and a white gauze scarf sewn with crystals disposed about her charge's shoulders, she handed Elizabeth her gloves and her fan and nodded grimly.

"It's not what I was wanting," she announced, "but you'll not be a speak for the whole town as I was first thinking. But I don't know what himself will be saying to it."

Hector, however, did not seem unduly shocked by the absence of silks, satins and lace.

"Lord, Liz, but you do look cool and comfortable," he remarked. "Tell me, is my collar wilting already?"

The storm had still not broken when dinner was served and neither of them could eat very much. Hector was silent and seemed rather *distrait* so Elizabeth did not try to make conversation.

As they were leaving, Hector looked enquiringly at Jacques who shook his head.

"Nothing has come for M'sieu ... nothing at all."

"Remember, if anything comes while I'm out have it brought to me at once. Better bring it yourself and be as quick as you can about it. Here is a card to give the door-keepers."

By the time they were lining up with the other carriages which were setting down their glittering loads at the steps of the theatre, the sky had become overcast and from time to time a distant flash was followed by an even more distant mutter of thunder. When their turn came Hector handed her out and they went up the steps into the vast foyer. They were soon absorbed into a chattering group and while Elizabeth exchanged observations on the heat and the personalities present Hector slipped away for a moment and Elizabeth saw him speak to one of the elaborately bewigged and liveried footmen who guarded the approaches to the auditorium. A coin changed hands and the man nodded enthusiastically. Hector rejoined the group and replied light-heartedly to enquiries about his health.

"I'm quite myself again, thank you."

He caught Elizabeth's eye and gave her an almost imperceptible wink.

Gradually the chattering crowd began to stir and swirl away through the doorways and up the superb staircase to take their seats. Hector and Elizabeth had places in one of the Embassy boxes. A flourish of trumpets announced the arrival of the President and his guests and the crowded house rose to receive them. The conductor appeared, bowed to the presidential box, raised his baton and swept the orchestra into the Marseillaise. When it was over the light began to dim as the army of footmen turned down the gas-lamps and the huge audience settled down to listen to the overture.

Just as the curtain was rising on the first scene the door of the box opened and one of the footmen came in and whispered to Hector who rose at once, muttered an apology and went out. Elizabeth felt her heart start to beat hard and found it difficult to concentrate on what was going on on the stage. The scene had not been playing for more than a few minutes when the door opened again and another footman appeared. There was a movement of irritation from the woman who sat beside Elizabeth. The man whispered,

"Madame Lacombe?"

Elizabeth turned her head in surprise. He bowed and

handed her a note. It was hard to read in the light from the stage but as the writer had had the foresight to write it in capital letters she managed to decipher it.

"I MUST SPEAK TO YOU AT ONCE. IT CONCERNS THE LITTLE ONE. IT IS MOST IMPORTANT. PLEASE COME. I AM IN THE FOYER.
EDOUARD MASSIN."

The rest of the party were by now engrossed in the opera or pretending to be, so that Elizabeth could rise and slip out quietly without comment. As she closed the door she blessed the impulse which had led her to leave off the crinoline. Such an unobtrusive exit would have been impossible with a seven-foot hoop.

The foyer was all but deserted. Two footmen were talking behind one of the pillars and one of them came forward to meet her.

"Madame Lacombe? The gentleman is waiting for you in one of the offices."

He led the way down a corridor, tapped on a door, opened it and bowed her inside.

By this time the coming storm had dimmed the daylight to an early dusk and Elizabeth could scarcely see the waiting figure seated in the window. He did not rise as she came in. The door clicked to behind her.

"Ah, Madame ... a pleasure to meet you again so soon," said the figure in the window and she realised at once that it was not Massin but de Mavanne. The palms of her hands were suddenly wet.

"I thought it was high time we had some private conversation. We have a lot to discuss, you know."

"I have no desire to have any conversation with you at all, M'sieu. Will you please allow me to return to my seat."

De Mavanne did not answer. He rose and picked up an

object from the window seat. Elizabeth with an icy sensation in her stomach realised that it was a knife.

"I feel that this place is not private enough. We will find a more secluded spot."

"I will do nothing of the sort."

"Yes, Madame, you will because if you make the least commotion I will use this."

He moved swiftly across the room and took her arm, gripping it under his own with cruel fierceness. With his other hand he put the knife under his coat and pressed it, firmly enough to be uncomfortable, on her side, just above her waist.

"Now, Madame, open the door. We will walk across the foyer arm in arm like the old friends we are. And I warn you if you try to alert anyone I will press this home."

The knife-blade pierced the cambric of her stays with a little audible noise and she felt the point on her skin.

Once they were through the foyer into the deserted corridors beyond de Mavanne quickened his pace. They passed through one door and then another and then up four flights of stone stairs, dimly lit at rare intervals by hissing gas-jets. At length they arrived at a door not quite a quarter of the way along a long corridor.

"Knock!" said de Mavanne.

It was opened by Polichon who seemed out of breath. De Mavanne pulled her inside quickly and the door was shut and locked by Polichon. De Mavanne released Elizabeth.

"Give me the key. Did you send my message?"

"I did."

"Was it in time?"

"In plenty of time. He'd no chance to say a word."

"Excellent. Open the window and let's see what we must do."

While they were talking Elizabeth looked around the room. It was long and narrow and immensely high, and lit by two high narrow windows which seemed to give on to a balcony. In the gloom Elizabeth could just see part of an elaborate balustrade and the rigid gesture of a statue which stood upon it. She realised that they must be high on the front of the theatre for she remembered noticing the row of stone figures which adorned the upper storey. The room was full of boards, bits of scenery and decrepit theatrical properties.

Polichon struggled with the catch of the window until the long glass door swung inwards, groaning on its hinges. Just at that moment there was a blinding blue flash and a clap of thunder which shook the whole building. Polichon leaped back.

"Blessed saints! But that was close."

"The heavens foretell the death of princes," said de Mavanne drily, "or so they say. It's a good omen. Close that till we need to have it open. It will pour with rain in a minute."

Polichon obeyed and then vanished into the gloom at the far end of the room. De Mavanne indicated a heap of discarded curtains against the wall.

"Sit down," he said. "You've got a long wait ahead of you."

Elizabeth stood her ground.

"Why have you brought me here?"

"As a hostage," he said.

"A hostage for what?"

De Mavanne uncovered a shabby gilt and velvet footstool which he placed beside the window so that he could look down on to the road outside the theatre.

"A hostage for the good behaviour of your much too busy and curious husband. If he tells the wrong people

164

what he knows, he'll find you in the alley-way outside this theatre with your throat cut, another victim of the lamentable street violence in Paris. For your own sake you had better hope that the President comes into range tonight."

"What do you mean?"

He jerked his head at the object which Polichon had unearthed from the piles of rubbish at the other end of the room. Elizabeth realised it was a gun.

"A sporting rifle from London. Remarkably accurate at short range," said de Mavanne. "And Polichon is a remarkable shot. Are you not, Polichon?"

The man nodded and began to load the rifle.

"This room provides an excellent vantage point. Come here."

He pulled her over to the window.

"See. At this point the building is set forward over six feet in front of the facade. Given the excellent light provided by the lamps over the steps Polichon should be able to do his business comfortably. It isn't so sure a method as the one I had hoped to employ but ..."

There was another flash and a peal of thunder. Elizabeth shrank back and de Mavanne laughed.

"Thunder will do you no harm."

Elizabeth sat down on the heap of curtains. It smelt disgustingly of dust and mice.

"And afterwards?" she enquired calmly.

"Afterwards?"

He seemed slightly taken aback.

"After you have murdered the President?"

"We have arranged for a cab to be waiting in an alley. We should be in safety within a very few minutes."

"We?"

"Yes. You as well. We must keep your husband quiet until any noise he makes will not matter."

Elizabeth's mind was racing. It was fairly clear that neither she nor Hector were to survive this incident. They both of them knew too much. She would be the bait, live or dead, which would bring Hector into their trap.

"It's intolerably close in here," she remarked calmly, "perhaps you could open the window a crack."

De Mavanne shrugged and pulled at it so that it creaked open about a foot. The sound of music drifted in and Elizabeth realised that the opera had reached the end of the first act. De Mavanne yawned and reached into his breast-pocket, laying the knife across his knees. He produced a cigar and lit it.

"You will permit me to smoke, Madame," he said casually, "we have a long time to wait. Opera is for me an interminable form of art."

Elizabeth leaned back against the wall and tried to think how she might escape, but her thoughts resolved themselves into a constant silent repetition of Hector's name.

"Ah," said de Mavanne suddenly, "here comes the rain. That will clear the air a trifle."

It came battering and splashing on to the balcony and a breath of cool air crept into the room. By now it was so dark she could see nothing but the silhouettes of the two men occasionally lit dramatically by the lightning flashes.

Polichon stiffened suddenly and went to the door where he listened intently. Footsteps could be heard coming along the corridor. De Mavanne was across the room like a cat and had the knife across Elizabeth's throat.

"One sound from you ..." he breathed.

The footsteps came closer and a voice could be heard humming drunkenly a phrase from the opera. They stopped at intervals and doors were heard opening and shutting. They stopped at last outside the door of the room. The handle was rattled. Somebody muttered a curse when it would not open and the footsteps retreated again, rather unsteadily.

"Some drunken fool who's missed his way back to his seat," said Polichon and went back to polishing the rifle.

De Mavanne released Elizabeth and returned to his seat by the window. All Elizabeth could see was the glow of his cigar. The music began again.

When the second act began Hector was standing at one end of the long portico of the theatre. His face looked grim but to a casual glance he might have been a theatre-goer taking a much-needed breath of the fresh air. He had a cigar between his fingers but it had long since gone out. A shadowy figure sidled up the portico steps and crouched down behind one of the pillars to be out of the rain.

"M'sieu got my message?"

Hector did not turn his head.

"Yes."

He flung the dead cigar far out into the glistening street

"They have taken my wife," he said, "if the President is warned and does not appear after the performance . . . they mean to kill her."

The man behind the pillar whistled softly.

"That is a bad business."

Hector did not answer.

"If I can be of service, M'sieu ..."

"Thank you, Dodon. You can. Jacques has gone to see if he can find out where they have taken her."

The rain hammered and leaped along the road. A cab, with the driver muffled against the rain clopped by and turned down the alley-way which ran down the side of the theatre. Jacques came trotting down the steps to join them.

"She must still be in the theatre," he said at once. "They were not seen to leave by any of the doors and the men in the foyer say that she went with someone who sounds like M'sieu de Mavanne along the corridor which takes one to the upper circle staircase. They looked very friendly, they said, arm in arm."

Hector moved impatiently.

"I went there, M'sieu. I think that they are above us. In one of the rooms behind the balcony there."

He indicated the row of statues with a jerk of his chin. Hector gave them a quick searching look.

"I walked along the length of the corridor," said Jacques. "All the doors are open, save one."

"Which?"

"It must be the one which is behind the part where the balcony comes forward, there."

Again the jerk of the chin.

"More than likely," said Hector, thoughtfully, "they would have an excellent view of the departure from there. The balusters are like loopholes. Did you hear anything?"

"No, M'sieu. I was singing, you understand ... and a trifle unsteady upon my feet."

Dodon gave an admiring exclamation.

"He is a veritable fox, this one ..."

"But I smelt them. One in that room smokes a cigar."

"Ah!" breathed Hector, softly, "Dodon ..."

"At once, M'sieu."

The little pickpocket shambled across the street and began to move down the pavement on the other side. In a few minutes he appeared again on their side and came quickly to where they were standing.

"M. Jacques is right. The third window from the end is

168

a little open. There is a man sitting just inside it. I saw him by a lightning flash."

"You are sure?"

"As I live," Dodon said earnestly. "Can we not climb along the balcony, creep to the window and surprise the sons of unspeakable mothers?"

"No," said Hector sharply.

"With Madame in their hands?" reproved Jacques," it is to invite disaster. No, I have a better plan. Does M'sieu care to hear it?"

Hector nodded.

"It would need care, but it might give an opportunity."

He outlined a plan. Dodon applauded softly.

"A fox, a fox!" he declared, "with the heart of a lion, one perceives."

But Hector was uncertain about one important aspect.

"But M'sieu, you have no choice in the matter," said Jacques reasonably, "I cannot play your part in the scheme ... I am too old and too fat ... and you are by far too tall to play mine. And M'sieu we are wasting time. It will require all we have to persuade them that we are speaking the truth and then to arrange matters."

After an hour or so the rain eased and the sky cleared. Elizabeth saw a star or two between the chimney pots. The room by now was chilly and she shivered in her thin muslin. The two figures at the window hardly moved a muscle. The last act of the opera began. Twice an aria was encored and both men muttered impatiently. At last a clatter of hooves was heard and the presidential carriage with its array of outriders drew up outside the portico. The noise of a gathering crowd drifted up through the window. The final chorus of the opera rose to its climax and was followed by prolonged applause. At this, the two men moved silently into action.

The window was pushed open as far as it would go and Polichon crawled out on to the balcony where he lay full length. De Mavanne handed him the rifle and he pushed the barrel between the balusters at the point where the balcony turned the angle of the building. He settled himself, grumbling under his breath at the puddles and sighted along the barrel, shifting and inching himself about until he had the right position. De Mavanne then came across to Elizabeth and pulled her roughly to her feet.

"Now, girl, you know what will happen to you if you make a sound."

He hauled her over to the window where he took up his position just inside, where he could command a view past the statue which adorned the corner of the balcony. He held her in front of him, her arm twisted painfully behind her back and the knife pressed hard into her right side.

"You had better pray hard that your husband thinks more of you than he does of the President," said Mavanne. "You'll know what to think if the man appears ... but if he doesn't you won't have much time to repine, I promise you."

The knife dug into her. He fell silent and they watched the scene outside the portico with a painful intensity. Elizabeth could feel de Mavanne's heart beating hard, and wondered idly if he realised how frightened she was for the same reason.

The soldiers of the bodyguard emerged and lined the steps, pushing the crowd back. There was a growing sound of cheering. De Mavanne pressed forward to see better until Elizabeth was nearly on the balcony. She smelt him sweating and her throat closed with nausea. She pushed her head forward to breath more easily. To the left of the window a flicker of movement caught her eye, as if one of the statues had moved. She caught her breath, but de

Mavanne, his eyes intent on the entrance, had noticed nothing. She glanced along again, without moving her head and this time there could be no mistake. Someone, no, several people were closing in on them along the balcony.

Polichon gave a curious little grunt, there was a burst of waving and cheering and cries of, *"Napoléon! Vive l'Empire!"* A diminutive figure in evening dress had emerged from the theatre and was waving and bowing to the crowd from the top of the steps. A muffled exclamation burst from de Mavanne when the figure was engulfed in the escort as he moved slowly down the steps. The crowd closed round the carriage and de Mavanne cursed again. He craned forward and Elizabeth felt the pressure against her side ease. Her left hand was numbed with the grip on her wrist but she knew that the grip had relaxed just a trifle. The little plump figure below them bobbed and emerged head and shoulders above the crowd as he mounted the step of the carriage.

"Now!" breathed de Mavanne and Elizabeth lunged sideways away from the knife, her left arm slipping out of his sweating hand. She kicked hard at Polichon and heard the shot echoing along the street. As she did this a shadow plunged out of the darkness between her and the cursing de Mavanne. She stumbled over Polichon, lost her balance and fell, striking her head hard on the balustrade. The lights in the street below spun into a vast catherine-wheel and exploded into blackness.

13

Hector took the bowl of broth from Catriona's hands.

"Revenge at last!" he gloated and sat down beside the bed. "When I think of the amount of this stuff you spooned into me a few weeks ago ..."

Elizabeth chuckled and winced slightly.

"I am perfectly capable of feeding myself," she announced.

"Massin says you are to rest for a day or two," he returned, "and rest you will."

He began to spoon the broth into her mouth. Catriona squealed with dismay as it ran down the patient's chin and lost itself among the pillows and she would not let him continue till she had placed a protective screen of towels and napkins around Elizabeth's bandaged head. She then watched his inexpert efforts for a minute, cast up her eyes to heaven and left the room.

"This is really great nonsense," remarked Elizabeth between spoonfuls, "there's nothing wrong with me except a broken head."

"Massin says you must be suffering from some degree of strain from such an ordeal, and so ..."

He presented another spoonful.

"It is really Jacques you ought to be feeding," she said when she had swallowed it, "that must have been a strain if you like. I mean, to walk out there and *know* that there was a gun or something just waiting ..."

"Jacques has borne up remarkably well," Hector informed her, "and he has had a lot to bear. He has been kissed on both cheeks by the President and invested with the Legion d'Honneur on the spot ... and I think from what the secretary said to me he is to get something a little more substantial than that. Then there was the scene when we got back here."

"To think I missed all this."

"Catriona had heard the story from Dodon ... and I don't suppose it lost anything in the telling ... so when Jacques and I eventually came home she greeted him by falling on his neck. It was a most touching affair. Jacques wept too."

"Oh, put that horrid bowl away," she begged, "I detest chicken broth of all things. Tell me all about everything."

"Massin said you were to go straight to sleep. He left you a draught."

"How can I go to sleep until I know what happened?"

He looked doubtfully at the door.

"Oh, very well ... but Catriona will pull my ears for me if she catches me."

He measured out the drops into a glass, put his arm under her pillows and lifted her head so that she could drink.

"There. Now where do I start?"

"Ugh! To think I forced this horrid stuff down your throat every night. I wonder you didn't throw it at me."

"I came near to it once or twice. Where would you like me to begin?"

"What happened after you got the message from de Mavanne?"

"Jacques went to see what had happened to you and found out where you were."

"Was he the drunk man in the corridor?"

"He was."

"I have never known him at a loss."

"No, thank God. The whole plan was his, you know. To warn the President and then take his place so that we could surprise them during the attempt to shoot him when their attention was on him and not so much on you. Dodon was all for going in right away."

"Thank goodness you didn't," she shuddered, "that knife ... he really would have used it I think."

"I am sure he would," said Hector grimly, "and that is why we did what Jacques suggested. Even that put you at risk. When you fell I thought you'd been shot ..."

"Instead of tripping over my own stupid feet," she observed sleepily, "imagine being unconscious while you were dealing with them. What did happen to them?"

"De Mavanne fought," said Hector, not without satisfaction, "but we had taken him by surprise. He tried to get away along the balcony but we had people along both sides and rather than be taken he ..."

He stopped and looked at her doubtfully.

"Oh, don't worry about my sensibilities," she said, "I suppose he jumped. I'm glad I didn't see that."

"So am I. Polichon wasn't much trouble. After we had fought on top of him he was so battered and dazed that he went with the gendarmes like a lamb. And that was all really. After that I got you home."

"And Jacques?"

"Jacques drove to the presidential home in state. And there he was met by the real President who had gone home earlier by cab from a side door. I'll say this for Louis-Napoleon ... he was quite ready to do it himself. It was a hard task to persuade him to let Jacques take his place."

"I really thought it was the President. Where did he get his beard and moustache?"

"Where do you think? Backstage."

"Of course."

Elizabeth was fighting to keep her eyes open.

"I wonder what they'll say at the Embassy," she remarked.

"Time enough to worry about that."

He pulled the sheet up over her shoulders and turned down the lamp. When he turned back to the bed she was asleep. He looked at her for a minute and then bent over and kissed her. When he straightened up Catriona was on the other side of the bed.

"She's asleep," he said, rather unnecessarily.

"Aye," said Catriona, "but she'll mebbe be awake next time."

Lord Normanby called next morning. He was apologetic, solicitous and congratulatory by turns before he told Elizabeth that she and Hector were to have leave to go back to England almost at once. He hinted that it would be embarrassing to have a member of the Embassy staff a prominent witness during the trials which were bound to follow such an attempt. Hector was to make a full statement concerning what he had discovered before he left and his name was to be kept out of the proceedings as far as possible.

It was not until just before he took his leave that Elizabeth realised that she would not be coming back to Paris.

"And of course this is bound to be a great feather in his bonnet. He's almost sure to be promoted. More than a chance they'll send him to Washington. Fillingham's been sent home sick. How will you like America, do you think?"

She was still digesting this piece of news when Jacques and Catriona came together into the little parlour. It became clear that it was going to be an unusual kind of interview when Catriona took one look at her mistress and burst into noisy tears. Jacques with a long-suffering expression on his face patted her kindly on the shoulder and told her to run along and return when she was more composed. Catriona gave a long Celtic wail and departed.

"Jacques, what on earth is all this about?"

Jacques looked faintly embarrassed.

"It is this way, Madame. We desire to be married, the good Catriona and I."

"Married! But you haven't exchanged a civil word in six months!"

Jacques took this broadside with dignity.

"Nevertheless, Madame, we have discovered that ... we ... that we have a mutual regard for one another."

Elizabeth could think of nothing to say. She simply stared. Jacques' eyes twinkled.

"I can understand that it might come as a slight surprise to you."

"I imagine you can. When I think of what Catriona has called you ..."

He held up a hand.

"This is a thing of the past, she assures me," he said solemnly, and then added with a wry smile, "and if I do not altogether believe her, what would you? It is what makes her herself, you understand."

Elizabeth, remembering certain scenes in which Catriona had played her part could only nod agreement.

"But the meat of the matter is this, Madame. She has agreed to be my wife but only if you will consent to let

176

her go. If you still have need of her she will stay single all her days."

Elizabeth could hear her say it.

"But I think she has realised that you no longer depend on her as once you did. This gives me hope."

"As if I would stand in her way."

"Hush, Madame. You must not put it that way. You must part with her reluctantly, grudgingly, or she will never leave you at all!"

For the second time in the interview Elizabeth was left speechless. All she could do was laugh, so she did and Jacques smiled approvingly.

"I see Madame understands the situation perfectly. We shall do. Now to more practical matters. She would like you to attend the ceremony of course, so we must hurry matters so that we can be married before you leave for England."

"But how did you know? I only knew myself a few minutes ago."

Jacques regarded her pityingly.

"But it was obvious to the meanest intelligence, Madame. M'sieu could not stay in Paris after such an *affaire*. Later he may return, not much later as I judge, but he must go away now."

"I see," said Elizabeth, humbly. "But I do not see why the wedding must be hurried on. Will you not come with us to England?"

"Alas, no, Madame. My opportunity has come and I must seize it. His Highness has very graciously ordered that I be given a sum of money for the slight service I did him."

"And me," interrupted Elizabeth feelingly.

Jacques bowed.

"Madame is kind. I should explain that it has been my

177

intention to open a small hotel when I had saved sufficient money. Now I can do this. You are leaving and have no further need of my services in Paris and I do not think I could be happy in England."

"We shall be sorry to lose you, Jacques, but I am delighted that you can do what you want. Catriona would enjoy helping you in such a scheme I think."

"She has already planned our establishment, down to the pattern on the china and the colour of the curtains," admitted Jacques, "whereas I have certain ideas as to cuisine ..."

"But Catriona cannot cook!" Elizabeth exclaimed, "She has no ideas beyond herring and porridge."

Jacques shrugged.

"One cannot have everything in this world, Madame. And I am myself proficient."

"Naturally."

"Madame mocks herself at me," Jacques diagnosed good-humouredly.

"As if I would dare," said Elizabeth. "I congratulate you, Jacques, and wish you both every happiness."

He bowed his thanks.

"And Jacques, you must tell us what you would like most for your hotel so that we can give it to you for a wedding present."

"Madame has already given me what I desired most," he returned, "a notable housekeeper. But it would give us both pleasure if you would perhaps honour us by staying in the hotel, some time when your duties permit."

"Of course. As soon as possible."

"And now Madame must retire to rest. Catriona will expect you upstairs without delay. Your luncheon will be brought to your room."

Elizabeth was about to obey meekly and pass in front of him out of the room when he coughed gently.

"There is just one matter ..."

"Yes, Jacques?"

"The good Catriona has said ... it is the custom in her village for there to be a piper ... have I that correctly ... at every wedding."

Elizabeth recalled her father's tales of Island weddings.

"Yes, this is true. He plays the bridegroom to the door and plays for the guests in the bride's father's house."

"She would very much like to have a piper. Women have their fancies at such times. But I do not at all know where I may find such a person."

"You, of all people, to be at a loss, Jacques! I never thought to see it. I'll speak to my husband. He may be able to find one."

Early in August Elizabeth and Hector boarded the night steamer at Calais. The last days in Paris had been passed in a flurry of activity which had culminated in the wedding of Jacques and Catriona. This combined something of the splendours of both French and Island weddings for Hector had obtained a piper. This gentleman had remained in Paris after the occupation in 1815 in circumstances which did not bear close investigation, but he possessed the attributes of a true piper, a kilt, a set of magnificent military pipes and an inordinate capacity for liquor. The French guests listened bemused to the noises he produced as he marched about the board which was lavishly spread with viands unmistakably French. Catriona wept unceasingly and bemoaned the absence of the whisky which graced weddings in her part of the world. The guests sympathised but drank the excellent wine with a certain relief, thinking that the liquor of *ces Ecossais sauvages*

179

might well be like their music ... almost insupportable.

After the wedding the newly-married pair had departed to Jacques' birthplace in the south where they were to prospect for a suitable venue.

"And remember, mo chridhe, if you are wanting Catriona I will be coming at once," Catriona said tearfully at the station. "Even if I have to be crossing the sea in a boat!"

Elizabeth again addressed herself to the task of convincing her that she could exist without her ... just. Catriona then adjured Hector at length to look after Elizabeth in terms which would have given any bystander to understand that she was still a baby in arms. Hector solemnly promised to be mindful of his duties while Elizabeth flushed with fury.

"Och, och and I would have liked it fine to have seen her with a wee one of her own before I was leaving here."

With a wicked sideglance at Elizabeth Hector promised that he would endeavour to oblige her in this as well. His wife tried beyond endurance lost her temper.

"And why," she demanded in the Gaelic, "if you are so wanting wee ones should you not have some of your own? You're a young woman yet ... and Jacques is capable of anything! I'll be looking for a letter from you before long!"

It was Catriona's turn to blush and scold Elizabeth for being too free with her tongue and her a young lady. Hector and Jacques listened fascinated to the incomprehensible exchange.

"I can see, Jacques," Hector remarked, "that we will have to learn Gaelic."

Jacques blenched at this proposition but Catriona called from the window of the carriage as the train moved out of the station.

"You could be doing worse. It's a grand tongue for swearing and for loving and you'll be needing both for that one!"

Elizabeth stood stiffly on the platform not daring to look at Hector.

"And that one would sell her soul to have the last word!" she declared furiously.

Hector had just laughed and signalled for a cab in which Elizabeth had sat silent and on her dignity for fully two minutes before she too had begun to laugh.

At Calais they were greeted with a squall of wind and rain. Outside the harbour the sea was rough and threatening with white-caps flecking the surly grey. Even in the harbour the little steamer in which they were to cross heaved slightly.

"The English weather begins at Calais, I see," remarked Hector as they went aboard. "It looks as if we are going to have a lively crossing. Just as well that Catriona isn't here."

Elizabeth did not answer at once. Catriona's frank comments had helped to intensify the tension which had recently grown up between Hector and herself. In the bustle of departure, packing up and closing the house, this tension had been ignored, but during the journey in which they had been thrown into one another's company she had become more and more conscious of him. Their exchanges had become stilted and stiff and the easy cameraderie which they had enjoyed after his illness had gone. She knew well enough what was the matter. No one brought up by Catriona could remain a bread-and-butter Miss. It was just that she did not know how to mend matters. The circumstances of their marriage had been such that the next move must be hers and she did not

181

know how to make it. And with a Clothilde in the offing she was uncertain whether she should consider making it at all.

"You look uncommonly serious," Hector interrupted her thoughts. "Are you having internal qualms already?"

She denied this indignantly and they strolled aft to watch the preparations for departure. The steamer's lines were cast off, smoke belched from the tall smokestack, showering the deck with smuts and the little vessel churned her way out of the harbour entrance. Almost at once she buried her bow in a steep sea, plunged and pitched so that the passengers still on deck staggered and clutched at the rail to steady themselves. Out of the shelter of the harbour the wind was chilly and the rain beat on their faces. It was beginning to get dark.

"You're cold," said Hector. "We'll go below."

He helped her down the heaving companionway and they went into the saloon. It was completely deserted so they sat by the port-hole and watched the coast of France vanish into the dusk. Their conversation flagged and faltered. A steward came in and lit the lamps. He nodded approval at them.

"Good travellers, I see. Don't have many aboard this trip. You should see the lower deck, oh Lord!"

He cast his eyes up in mock despair.

"Can I fetch you summat before you turn in?" he asked, "soup, coffee, tea, brandy, glass o' wine for the lady ..."

He balanced easily on the heaving deck and smiled benevolently upon them. Hector looked enquiringly at Elizabeth.

"Some chicken-broth?" he suggested teasingly and she made a face at him.

"My dinner is still a happy memory," she told him, "but I'd like a glass of wine."

"Wine for the lady. And you, sir?"

"Brandy and water."

He came back at once balancing the glasses on a tray in one hand while he fitted fiddles to their table. Hector asked him when he thought they might make Dover.

"We'll be latish, sir, I reckon. The old Queen, she's safe and steady . . ."

He grabbed at the back of a chair as he spoke and the contents of Elizabeth's glass slopped on to the table.

". . . but she's not built for speed as you might say. If this headwind keeps up we'll miss the tide and have to wait outside a while."

"Let's hope it moderates, then."

"Doubt it, sir. Be worse before it's better, they say. But you'll not care for that, I daresay, you and your lady."

He smiled approval on them again.

"Just call me if you want anything further, sir. I'll not be far. Stukeley's the name."

By this time it was completely dark and the only thing to be seen through the port-hole was the spume from the paddles faintly illumined by the light from the saloon lamps.

"It looks as if we're in for a longish crossing," Hector remarked, after a short silence, "but we're in no hurry after all."

"No," said Elizabeth. "No hurry. What do we do after we've seen your father?"

"Whatever you like."

Hector leaned back and nursed his glass, looking at her.

"I don't know . . . I hadn't thought . . ."

"We could go to the Devon house with my father, if

you wanted. He'll be going for a month or so. You've never been to Lacombe Place, have you?"

She shook her head.

"It'll be ours some day. It's an old rambling place high on the cliffs above the sea. You'd like it I believe. Or we could go north. Wouldn't you like to see your father's people."

Elizabeth hesitated.

"Can't we go to Hampshire?" she said at last, "I would like to take Louisa ... before Joanna ... I mean, she's ours now, isn't she?"

There was a silence. Hector leaned forward.

"Are you certain you want to?" he asked very seriously.

"I am."

He looked at her steadily.

"You know, it wouldn't be difficult to find someone kind and decent who'd bring her up and look after her till she grew up. And after that, well, she's well-provided for."

"I promised," said Elizabeth, "I promised she'd be like my own."

"It isn't every woman," said Hector, very deliberately, "who would want a living reminder of her husband's peccadilloes about her house."

"It wasn't *like* that, Hector," she protested, "you know it wasn't."

"Yes, I know."

"Don't you want to have her? Will she be just a re-minder to you?"

"Yes, I want her. She's mine after all. Curious, to feel so possessive about a scrap you've never even seen."

"She's mine too," said Elizabeth flatly. "Eloise gave her to me."

There was a pause as the ship plunged and then pitched skittishly over a larger than average roller. Outside the

184

saloon the paddles bellowed their protest at such treatment before settling to their work again, deep in the water. The two glasses rolled unheeded on to the carpeted deck. Hector picked up Elizabeth's hand and held it to his cheek.

"You're a woman in a million, Liz, did you know that?"

He kissed her palm and stood up, somewhat uncertainly.

"We'll go to Hampshire and take her with us into Devonshire. I enjoyed being a child in Lacombe Place and I hope she will too. Does that please you?"

She nodded and found that she was trembling.

"Hector? Would you tell me something?"

"Of course."

"Who ... who is Clothilde?"

"Clothilde ... Good heavens, Liz, why? Of course, she came to the house, didn't she?"

Elizabeth blushed slightly.

"I just wondered ..."

He grinned mischievously at her.

"I don't know how to put it to a gently nurtured female," he said, "but she was a member of an elegant establishment on the Rue Bercy."

"I knew about the Rue Bercy. I didn't realise it was an establishment."

"Oh, a very high-class establishment indeed. No one admitted without money or a title. Clothilde had a very ... eminent ... clientele and a way of beguiling information from them which we found very useful. And she used the money to support her little boy."

"Had?"

"I'm afraid so. Clothilde has found a rich protector and is now suitably established in an *appartement meublé* and, I fear, finding life rather monotonous."

185

"I see," said Elizabeth. "I thought she was very pretty."

"Did you? A bit opulent for my taste."

"Oh?"

"To be perfectly open with you I will have to admit that she was 'recruited' so to speak by my unregenerate father on an earlier visit."

She giggled.

"I see."

"I hope you do. Come along. Time to·turn in."

They made their unsteady way aft, along the companionway to the cabins.

"I'm just next door," he told her, "knock on the wall, or whatever they call it on board ship, if you are ... if you need anything. Goodnight."

Elizabeth found herself alone in the cabin and sat down hastily upon the bunk. Quite apart from the violent motion of the ship, her legs were trembling and she felt as stormy and confused as the waters which churned past her porthole. Tears began to run down her cheeks.

"Idiot ... dolt ... baby ..." she apostrophised herself in a furious whisper, "I wish I knew what was the matter with me ..."

Catriona's mocking face floated for a second in some corner of her mind.

"What a piece of work to make about ... about *what*?"

She got up and began to make her preparations for bed by exploring the facilities provided by the steam-packet company. They were surprisingly complete. No need to face the journey to the uncomfortable apartment at the end of the companion. The stewardess had already laid out the contents of her night-bag. She took off her heavy linen travelling-dress and hung it on the hook where it swung gaily. Her petticoats were laid across the stool, and then, by dint of holding tightly to the brass rail, she succeeded in pouring out some water into the basin and washing off the dirt of the journey, slowly but thoroughly. Then she brushed her teeth and began to comb out her hair. Before she had completed the last task she was conscious of a wish that she had found someone to take Catriona's place before she left Paris.

This wish was intensified when, her hair in its plait, she attempted to take off her stays. They had no hooks in the front and were laced at the back. Régine, deputising for Catriona, had laced her into them that morning and then tied the tags in a neat bow over which she had knotted the loops. This elaborate fastening was situated in the one place on her back which it was quite impossible to reach, try as she would. She tried to twist the stays around to bring the fastening to a point where she could undo it, but Régine had taken her new duties seriously and they were much too tight to move. After five minutes struggle she realised that either she would have to sleep in them or ... she looked at the wall which separated her from Hector. A bone mishandled during her exertions had broken and was pressing painfully into her side and this made up her mind for her. She picked up her discarded shoe and knocked on the wall.

When Hector appeared at the door in his dressing gown, his hair all upon end, she was sitting on the bunk giggling helplessly.

"I can't untie them," she explained, "and I *won't* sleep in the horrid things. Would you mind?"

Hector regarded the cambric and whalebone contraption with an expression of horror which made her giggle again.

"I should think you couldn't sleep in that ... that ... instrument of torture. I'm surprised you can breathe. Turn round."

187

As he struggled with Régine's intricacies the heavy plait of her hair got in his way and he put it gently over her shoulder.

"Why do women wear such things?" he enquired. "Don't they hurt you?"

"You get used to them, in time. And men wear them too, you know. Haven't you heard Cousin Froggie creaking?"

The knot came undone at last and he began to loosen the lacing.

"He needs them. You don't."

His voice was constricted.

"Oh, *thank* you! What a relief! Régine put them on much too tight."

He helped her slip them down over the shift.

"There."

She stepped out of them and turned round to thank him. He smiled appreciatively at the figure in the thin silk and the moment seemed to stretch out and out . . .

At that point the ship, having cleared the coast, turned a few degrees south so that the wind was on her quarter. The pitching motion gave way to a cork-screwing roll. It took both of them by surprise. Elizabeth lost her grip on the upright of the bunk and staggered off-balance. Hector, flung sideways, tried to catch her and lost his footing so that they ended in an undignified heap on the deck of the cabin, laughing helplessly. Elizabeth made an effort to disentangle herself but Hector pulled her back into his arms and held her tightly. He had stopped laughing. After a few seconds he released her and looked into her face.

"Liz?" he began on a questioning note and did not go on. In answer she put her arms round his neck. He gave a little gasp and kissed her, gently at first and then with a growing passion which was quenched by another roll of the ship which sent them both sliding over the carpet to the door where they fetched up with a thump. He sat up anxiously.

"Of all the fools! Liz! Are you all right? Your head?"

Liz was laughing again.

"My head's fine ... if you'd just get your elbow off my braid ..."

He got unsteadily to his feet, using the door as a support and reached for her hand.

"You'd best get into your bunk. It's the only safe place when the ship's rolling like this."

"Safe!" she exclaimed, "I'll be pitched out!"

"I'll tuck you in tightly."

He chose his moment and lifted her swiftly across on to the bunk sitting down heavily beside her.

"And who is going to tuck you in?" she demanded as he began to pull at the blankets.

"I shan't need any," he replied ruefully. "I'll just wedge myself in. My bunk is at least six inches too short."

"In that case," she said, catching at his hand, "just you wedge yourself in here. It'll stop me falling out too."

He bent over her, his hand at her waist and she felt her heart beating up into her throat.

"You want me to stay? Really?"

"Very much," she whispered.

He bent over more closely and kissed the hollow of her shoulder, and Elizabeth put her hand behind his head, stroking the thick springy dark hair. For a long moment he stayed like that and then sat up and chuckled.

"Conditions are not what you might call ideal," he observed, reaching to turn down the lamp in the bracket above the bunk, "but I'm sure Catriona would be impressed."

189

HERE COMES A CANDLE
Jane Aiken Hodge

Here is a fine novel of romance, betrayal and mystery.

When the Americans sacked the English capital of Canada at the out-
break of the war of 1812, Kate Croston, newly widowed and seemingly
lost, was only too glad to flee her shadowed past and accept the offer of
help given by an American civilian, Jonathan Penrose.

But as soon as she became the charge of Jonathan's daughter, little
Sarah, Kate found herself caught in a web of intrigue and suspicion.

Was Jonathan wise to defy his arrogant wife, Arabella, and place Sarah
in Kate's care?

And what was the role of the handsome Englishman, Captain Manning-
ham, in this affair?

It was only when Arabella showed that she would stop at nothing –
even kidnapping her own daughter – to get at her husband's fortune
and when the war suddenly became one that was intensely close to all
their aspirations, that the mystery came into the open.

"Highly entertaining and diverting . . . anyone who enjoys full-blooded
historical novels will certainly enjoy this one" – *The Times Scotsman*

"Historical story served up with suspense and generously spiced with
intrigue and romance" – *Evening Standard*

A ROSE FOR VIRTUE
Norah Lofts

Hortense Beauharnais – a French princess, answerable to no–one but Napoleon

The post-Revolution years saw France in a state of flux, with the balance
of power shifting back to the bourgeoisie. No-one's rise to power was
more meteoric than that of Napoleon Bonaparte, a successful young
general when we first meet him here.

Hortense Beauharnais suddenly finds herself rubbing shoulders with
royalty as her mother remarries to beome Bonaparte's wife. As Napoleon struggles for power on the battlefields of Europe, so Hortense
charts her way through the French court – a chessboard world where
the motives are jealousy and greed and the prizes are thrones of con-
quered countries.

Despite attempts to retain her gay individuality, Hortense finds herself
married to Napoleon's brother Louis, but her heart is with Charles de
Flahaut, a gallant young officer. Unwilling to cross her stepfather,
plagued by epilepsy and assassination attempts, Hortense must wait
and see if time will take her to her lover.

THE PEACEABLE KINGDOM

Jan De Hartog

The engrossing bestseller about the growth and life of the Quaker Movement

Book 1: The Children of the Light

It began in Lancashire one summer afternoon in 1652 when two horsemen blundered into the quicksands of Morecambe Bay. One of the horsemen was George Fox, and one of those close to him at that time was Margaret Fell. From the passionate meeting of these two grew the Religious Society of Friends and the seeds of Quaker history were sown.

Fox lived and preached the Word in a violent, turbulent society. Cromwell never cared overmuch for non-Conformists; and in their turn Royalists and republicans alike went to great lengths in their efforts to degrade and humiliate the new breed of believers. But the courage, the strength in the face of fantastic persecution, the love and respect these people felt for each other – they were already brightly present, laying the foundations for further glory and further involvement in the years ahead.

Book 2: The Holy Experiment

The Children of the Light had been born; now came the Holy Experiment.

In 1681, a group of Quakers, led by William Penn, had sailed to America. There it was that they eventually founded their first settlement in what is now the city of Philadelphia. The community grew and prospered; some made vast fortunes and raised large families; they lived in considerable comfort and employed slaves. They made pacts with the Indians. They subdued the wilderness and turned it to their own uses.

But with wealth had come difficulties. Success bred complacency and the aims of the founders came to be eroded and ignored. And it was only through pain that many discovered that the quality of living can so often be more important than the standard of life.

"A huge novel which may very well take its place in scale and scope beside *Gone with the Wind* as a landmark in American fiction" – *Literary Guild Mazagine*.

"Brimful of magnificent, vigorous characters, struggling and loving and plotting and all but rising off the page to move the reader" – *Book-of-the-Month Club News*

THE PRESENT MASTERS OF THE PAST: FROM CORONET

JAN DE HARTOG
The Peaceable Kingdom:

☐	16656 8	Bk 1 The Children of Light	50p
☐	16874 9	Bk 2 The Holy Experiment	50p

JANE AIKEN HODGE

☐	10734 0	Here Comes a Candle	35p
☐	12790 2	The Winding Stair	35p
☐	16228 7	Greek Wedding	35p
☐	16465 4	Maulever Hall	35p

MARTHA ROFHEART

☐	16530 8	Cry "God for Harry"	50p

NORAH LOFTS

☐	15111 0	The King's Pleasure	35p
☐	16216 3	Lovers All Untrue	30p
☐	16950 8	A Rose for Virtue	35p

CATHERINE GAVIN

☐	04354 7	The Moon into Blood	40p
☐	15116 1	The House of War	40p

ANYA SETON

☐	02713 4	Avalon	35p
☐	01951 4	The Winthrop Woman	40p
☐	02469 0	Dragonwyck	35p
☐	02488 7	Foxfire	35p
☐	15683 X	The Mistletoe and Sword	30p

MARY STEWART

☐	15133 1	The Crystal Cave	40p

ROSEMARY SUTCLIFF

☐	15090 4	The Flowers of Adonis	40p

NIGEL TRANTER
Robert the Bruce Trilogy:

☐	15098 X	Bk 1 The Steps to the Empty Throne	40p
☐	16222 8	Bk 2 The Path of the Hero King	40p
☐	16324 0	Bk 3 The Price of the King's Peace	40p
☐	16466 2	Black Douglas	45p

DAVID WEISS

☐	12803 8	Sacred and Profane	75p
☐	15134 X	Naked Came I	50p
☐	15913 8	The Assassination of Mozart	50p

All these books are available at your bookshop or newsagent, or can be ordered direct from the publisher. Just tick the titles you want and fill in the form below.

CORONET BOOKS, P.O. Box 11, Falmouth, Cornwall.
Please send cheque or postal order. No currency, and allow the following for postage and packing:
1 book – 7p per copy, 2-4 books – 5p per copy, 5-8 books – 4p per copy, 9-15 books – 2½p per copy, 16-30 books – 2p per copy in U.K., 7p per copy overseas.

Name ....

Address...

....